Distraction has very strong arms.

"Okay. When you're ready," Leevi said.

Mo hesitated. It was one thing to jump into the arms of your coach, quite another to jump into the arms of—she might as well face it—an abundantly hot if annoyingly unreadable clubmate. But the look on his face was all business. For all intents and purposes, he *was* her coach. Kind of.

She took a deep breath of the frozen air and released it slowly, visualizing the muscles in her legs like coils, tightening, strength gathering for the moment of release. And then, keeping her sights focused ahead, she sprang up from the crouch and launched herself forward, body rigid, arms straight to her side, feet flexed and angled outward. Leevi caught her at the hips and held her above his head for several seconds before setting her gently to the ground.

"Good, but you need more power into it. Try it again."

Mo nodded. Okay. He wanted power? He'd get power. She crouched again, summoning every last ounce of strength in her body to jump up and out from the block. He caught her again, only let her down more slowly this time. Or was that just her imagination? Was it because her heart was doing a sprint around her chest, constricting her lungs so that she could hardly breathe? Was it because she *wanted* him to have set her down slowly?

When he set her on her feet, she took a shaky step backward. "How was that?" she managed to ask.

He blew out a breath. "Better."

The Finnish Line

Linda Gerber

speak
An Imprint of Penguin Group (USA) Inc.

Acknowledgments

Special thanks to Vic Method, Coach Casey Colby, and the athletes at WSJUSA, who were willing to answer even the lamest of questions, and who openly shared their insights and experiences with me. Your input was invaluable. Also to Coach Katheline Jongeling, in Lahti, Finland, who helped me experience the jumps firsthand. Best wishes in the Netherlands! As always, I could not write a word without the continuing support of my family; my YAs, Kate Coombs, Karen Dyer, and Marsha Skrypuch; and my Creative Supporters, Barb Aeschliman, Ginger Calem, Niccole Maggi, and Jen McAndrews. Thanks for your collective genius. *GUSH* And finally, deep, heartfelt thanks to my editor, Angelle Pilkington, whose guidance and wisdom I value beyond power of speech.

SPEAK
Published by the Penguin Group
Penguin Group (USA) Inc.,
345 Hudson Street, New York, New York 10014, U.S.A.
Penguin Group (Canada), 90 Eglinton Avenue East, Suite 700, Toronto, Ontario, Canada M4P 2Y3
(a division of Pearson Penguin Canada Inc.)
Penguin Books Ltd, 80 Strand, London WC2R 0RL, England
Penguin Ireland, 25 St Stephen's Green, Dublin 2, Ireland
(a division of Penguin Books Ltd)
Penguin Group (Australia), 250 Camberwell Road, Camberwell, Victoria 3124, Australia
(a division of Pearson Australia Group Pty Ltd)
Penguin Books India Pvt Ltd, 11 Community Centre, Panchsheel Park,
New Delhi - 110 017, India
Penguin Group (NZ), 67 Apollo Drive, Rosedale, North Shore 0745, Auckland, New Zealand
(a division of Pearson New Zealand Ltd)
Penguin Books (South Africa) (Pty) Ltd, 24 Sturdee Avenue, Rosebank,
Johannesburg 2196, South Africa

Registered Offices: Penguin Books Ltd, 80 Strand, London WC2R 0RL, England

Published by Speak, an imprint of Penguin Group (USA) Inc., 2007

1 3 5 7 9 10 8 6 4 2

CIP DATA IS AVAILABLE

SPEAK ISBN 978-0-14-240916-9

Printed in the United States of America

Dedicated to the Hyvinkää Tyttöt

The Finnish
Line

Lake Vesijärvi

Ski Park /
Lahti Ski
Museum

Mo's Lahti

Gallery Pro Puu

Church of the Cross

Lanu Sculpture Park

Lahden Upper Secondary School

Lahti Historical Museum

Application for the Students Across the Seven Seas
Study Abroad Program

Name: Maureen Clark
Age: 16
High School: Park City High School
Hometown: Park City, Utah
Preferred Study Abroad Destination: Finland

1. Why are you interested in traveling abroad next year?

Answer: I have always been interested in the Scandinavian culture and would love an opportunity to experience it firsthand in Finland.

(Truth: Finland just might be far enough away from my overinvolved dad to give me the chance do something on my own for a change.)

2. How will studying abroad further develop your talents and interests?

Answer: As a competitve ski jumper, the opportunity to learn new training techniques would only serve to enhance my performance on the hills.

(Truth: Jumping in Finland is about the only thing someone in my family hasn't already done.)

3. Describe your extracurricular activities.

Answer: Ski jumping

(Truth: What else is there?)

4. Is there anything else you feel we should know about you?

Answer: I am an eager learner and open to new experiences.

(Truth: Just get me away from home!)

Chapter One

Maureen Clark juggled her ski bag and rolled her suit-case over the polished floors of the arrivals lobby in the Vantaa-Helsinki airport. Electricity hummed in the glass prisms overhead, echoing the vibrations of excitement in her bones. After all those months of waiting, she was really and truly here.

She scanned the crowd for the representative from the Scholar Athlete Exchange program who was supposed to be waiting for her. Her smile faltered when she didn't see anyone, but only for a second. The flight had come in nearly forty minutes early, so whoever was coming probably

hadn't had time to get there yet. No need to let it spoil the moment. She was sixteen, not six. She could wait.

She found the currency exchange booth and traded her dollars for euros and then bought a prepaid cell phone at the neighboring Nokia kiosk. Her dad had insisted she get one "in case of an emergency." Like she didn't know the real reason: control. He might have agreed to let her travel halfway around the world, but he still wanted to keep a leash on her. Since she was the youngest of seven kids—the baby of the family and one of only two girls—to say he was protective of her would be an understatement. Try smothering.

Whatever. She wasn't going to argue about anything that got her a cell phone. She found a phone with a text-messaging option and bought an international calling card so she could use the phone for her own "emergencies"— like keeping in touch with her best friend back home.

She glanced at her watch. Too early in Utah for calls, but she could still send a text. Finding a quiet corner, she pulled out the phone and quickly thumbed in a message to her friend Janessa.

am in will call @ 5 2night b there

A hand touched her shoulder and Maureen jumped, nearly dropping the phone. Behind her stood a man wearing a GoreTex jacket and a pinched expression on his face. "Maureen Clark?"

2

"Yes?"

His posture relaxed. "I was afraid we'd lost you. Arho Peltonen, coach of the SAE club. Sorry I was late." He extended his hand and she shook it.

"Hauska tutustua," she said in her best phrase-book Finnish. "Pleased to meet you."

His smile broadened. "Ah. You've been studying. Excellent. Shall we go? If you'd like to gather your things, I'll pull up the car."

And that's how Maureen Clark found herself standing alone outside an airport halfway around the world from her home in Park City, Utah... grinning like a fool.

In the darkness, Maureen could just make out the silhouettes of trees beyond the airport parking lot. It was only four-thirty in the afternoon, but already black as midnight. She'd been warned that January days in Finland were short, but she didn't care. Limited daylight she could get used to. The important thing was that she was here.

Twin beams of light skittered over the ice and snow as a sleek Volvo wagon crunched up to the curb. Coach Peltonen swung open his door and jumped out, hurrying around the front of the car to take Maureen's suitcase. "Right, then. In you go. I'll load the bags."

She slid onto the leather seat and adjusted her lap belt, watching him in the rearview mirror. So this was her coach for the next ten weeks. He was a little older than she'd expected, with gray, thinning hair and a face weathered by

years of sun and snow. Still, he moved with athletic grace as he fitted her suitcase and long skis into the bed of the wagon and slammed the door closed.

Behind the wheel once more, Coach Peltonen turned to her. "So."

"So," she replied.

"I was honored to see your name on our enrollment." He eased the car away from the curb. "I am a great fan of your father's."

The smile melted from her face. *Not here, too.* As if her huge family wasn't enough, Maureen's dad—the control freak—was a former Olympian who had parlayed his medals into a career of extreme ski movies and coaching. He ran a top-ranked ski school near Park City and had become something of a local celebrity. The kind of notoriety he generated was exactly what Mo had hoped to leave behind.

"Really," she said.

"Yes, yes." Coach Peltonen nodded. "Saw his final run in Innsbruck in 'seventy-six. Watched every one of his films."

"Uh-huh." She watched snowflakes swirl past the window and felt the long arm of her dad's shadow reaching out to reel her in. She stiffened. No. None of that. She hadn't come five thousand miles just to let his image dominate her life from afar.

"He's quite a man, your father. We often hear of his school. You must be very proud, Miss Clark."

She managed to give him a smile. "Please, Mr. Peltonen, my friends call me Mo."

He chuckled. "And my athletes call me Coach." The turn signal ticked rhythmically as he changed lanes. "Mo." He gave her a sidelong glance. "Yes, I think it suits you. No nonsense. Strictly business."

She didn't know how to respond to that, so she just stared out the window again. Frost clung to the glass in random sketchy swirls, catching the light of passing cars and obscuring the snow-shrouded trees that huddled along the roadside. It looked so cold out there, yet inside the car was so nice...so warm...She yawned.

"Oh, no you don't." Coach Peltonen poked her arm. "Make yourself stay awake until the local bedtime and you'll get over jet lag a lot quicker."

Mo stifled another yawn and shook herself. "So...how far is it to Lahti?"

"About an hour's drive. Should give us time to go over some of the details of the program since you weren't able to make it for orientation."

She grimaced. "Yeah, sorry about that." The other students and their host families had met together the night before. Mo hadn't been able to make it because she'd needed to stay in Utah for her older brother's wedding. "Thanks for making a special trip to the airport to get me."

"Not to worry. You'll make up for it in practice." He flashed another smile. "Now reach behind the seat and

grab the SAE folder, would you? It's that one on top there. Inside, you'll see a yellow paper…"

They spent the next half hour reviewing the rules for the athletes in the exchange program. It was nothing Mo hadn't already seen in the registration packet—no drinking, no drugs, ten o'clock curfew, treat the host families with respect, that kind of thing.

"So how many are in the program?"

"We have twenty-seven international athletes and about two dozen from local clubs. All of you will attend Lahden Upper Secondary School. It's not far from the Sports Center. The green paper lists your course schedule."

Mo riffled through the papers until she found the schedule. Just what she'd expected. Overview of Finland, computer science, and precalculus. "Um, Coach? It wasn't quite clear in the handbook…will they be teaching in Finnish?"

Coach Peltonen nodded. "All except the overview class. That's just for the international students, so it will be taught in English. But don't worry. You'll all be assigned native student escorts to help with the language in your other classes. I think you'll find, however, that communication won't be a problem. Most of the faculty and students speak at least passable English. Small country in a big world and all."

Mo was glad to hear that. Even though she had been

studying Finnish from the moment she signed up for the program, she still hadn't learned much.

"You will attend classes from eight to eleven," Coach Peltonen continued. "Training runs from noon until early evening—or later, depending on the day and how the club progresses. It might be a little difficult at first—"

Mo raised her brows. "Hey, I'm up for it. My club back home trains about three or four hours a day. This will just be stepping it up a notch."

"That's what I like to hear." He gave her an approving nod. "We've also planned some cultural activities during your stay. You'll find a sample itinerary on the pink paper."

Mo's smile faded as she looked over the preplanned schedule. Every possible moment was blocked in. "Wow," she murmured.

She closed the folder and felt her newfound freedom slipping away.

The coach kept up a running commentary all the way to Lahti, not that Mo paid much attention. She was way too tired. What was up with all the chatter, anyhow? Her dad had always said that Finns were silent, brooding types. Coach Peltonen seemed almost giddy. She would have preferred the silence.

Finally, they pulled off the road and into a parking lot bordered by tall apartment buildings. "You'll like the

Aalto family. They have a daughter about your age. Kirsti, her name is. Spent the summer in Japan as a S.A.S.S. exchange student a year or so ago, so she knows what it's like to be far from home, experiencing a different culture. I'm sure you two will get along famously."

Mo flinched at his choice of words. "So, which one is theirs?"

He pointed to the unit straight ahead.

She climbed out of the car and regarded her new home with satisfaction. The building had a contemporary flair with clean lines and elegant lighting—the polar opposite of her massive six-bedroom, glorified cabin of a house in Park City. Towering, snow-frosted pines surrounded the building so that it looked as if it had been dropped right in the midst of some New Age enchanted forest. This she could get used to.

But the cold! That was something else altogether. Already the hairs in her nose were so frozen that they prickled every time she breathed in and out. Her skin felt tight and raw. Shivers penetrated all the way to her spine.

"Welcome to Finland," Coach Peltonen said. "From now on, you wear a hat." He shouldered her skis and walked toward the front of the building. Mo grabbed the suitcase and followed. Its wheels squeaked over the snow as if rolling through Styrofoam.

Inside the lobby, she stomped the snow from her boots and looked around. Nice. Very nice. From the polished-

granite floors to the streamlined furniture and richly pan-
eled walls, the place oozed Scandinavian chic. A far cry
from her mom's homey cottage-style decor.

She and Coach Peltonen took the elevator to the fifth
floor.

"The Aaltos are in number 502," he said, leading the
way down the hall. "They should be expecting—"

At that moment, the door marked 502 swung inward to
reveal a tall, barrel-chested man with a ruddy complexion
and a salesman's smile. He must have stood at least six
nine and had the thick build of a Viking. "Ah! Maureen, is
it? *Tervetuloa!* Welcome to our home."

"Allow me to introduce you," Coach Peltonen said.
"Maureen, this is Mr. Aalto. And this"—he nodded at
Mo—"is Maureen Clark."

Mo inclined her head. *"Hauska tutustua, Herra Aalto."*

"Ah. *Hyvä!* Very good! I am pleased to meet you, too."
Herra Aalto's booming laugh echoed down the hallway.
He stepped aside and swept an arm toward the open door.
"Come in, come in."

Mo pushed her suitcase into the entry and parked
it against the wall next to a long bench. Several pairs
of shoes were lined up neatly underneath. She stole a
quick glance at Herra Aalto's stocking-clad feet. Crud.
She wished she had remembered that Finns didn't wear
shoes in the house. Mo's lucky socks—the ones she *had*
to wear on the flight—featured a hole just large enough

for her right big toe to poke through. She'd meant to sew it up before she left home, but with the wedding and her farewell party and packing and everything, she'd run out of time.

Coach Peltonen removed his shoes and followed Herra Aalto down the hallway. Mo quickly pulled off her boots and padded over the blond-wood floor behind them, curling her toes as she went.

In the front room, a tall girl wearing straw-colored braids and a Nordic sweater stood next to Herra Aalto. "Allow me to present my daughter, Kirsti."

Kirsti inclined her head. "*Hauska tutustua*. Pleased to meet you." But there was no warmth in her voice and her ice-blue eyes told Mo that Kirsti was far from pleased.

"Won't you have a seat?" Herra Aalto gestured to a low cream-colored sofa. He signaled to Kirsti, who dropped onto one of the matching chairs facing the couch.

Mo perched on the sofa, knees almost touching a heavy sculpted-glass coffee table. The thing looked like a big shaved-off chunk of ice with lines and bubbles running throughout the glass. Instinctively, she reached out and touched the glass.

"Do you like it?" Herra Aalto asked. "Had it specially made. Cost a king's ransom, I can tell you."

"It's very nice," Mo said. Kirsti caught her eye and smirked, looking pointedly past the table to where Mo's bright red toenail peeked through the hole in her dark blue sock. Mo curled her toes under again as a woman in a starched apron hurried into the room balancing a silver teapot, tea glasses, and a plate of small rolls on a tooled silver tray.

Mo's eyes widened. Wow. The Aaltos must be loaded. Servants and everything!

The woman set the tray on the coffee table and began filling the glasses with a pale pink liquid. Steam curled lazily upward, filling the air with a gentle scent of roses.

Herra Aalto settled in his chair, a proud smile on his face. "Eeva makes her own rose-hip tea. You must try it. It's quite delicious."

Mo accepted a glass and sipped dutifully as the woman hovered with an expectant look on her face. The stuff tasted like diluted perfume, but Mo smiled anyway. "It's very good. Thank you, Eeva."

Next to her, Coach Peltonen cleared his throat. Kirsti coughed. Mo looked from one to the other, face burning. Was it impolite to address the help? Or to call an older person by their first name?

Kirsti raised her glass. *"Kiitos, Äiti."*

Mo almost heard her jaw clunk when it hit the floor. Thank you, *Äiti*? That was the Finnish word for "mother." "Oh, I'm so sorry."

Mrs. Aalto—*Rouva* Aalto—smiled and nodded like it was no big deal, but Mo's face burned hotter than the tea in her glass. Way to make a good impression. The rest of

the conversation would be a goner. Mo sipped her tea in silence.

When Rouva Aalto invited everyone to come to the dinner table, Mo followed reluctantly. The combination of her less-than-stellar debut and her lack of sleep had killed her appetite. Besides, it may have been dinnertime in Finland, but back home she would just be getting up for breakfast. She picked at her meal—some sort of casserole served with crusty rye bread and lots of butter—and tried to act interested as Herra and Rouva Aalto droned on about the family's tour company and its first-quarter earnings.

Rouva Aalto said something in Finnish and Herra Aalto nodded. "You must be very tired," he said to Mo. "Are you ready to turn in?"

Coach Peltonen took his cue. "I should be going as well. Mo, enjoy your weekend. Rest up. School and practices begin on Monday."

As Herra Aalto walked the coach to the door, Mo stood and pushed her chair up to the table. "*Kiitos* for the dinner, Rouva Aalto. It was delicious."

Rouva Aalto beamed. "*Ei kestä.* You are very welcome."

At this, Kirsti rolled her eyes and stalked away down the hall. Mo watched her disappear and frowned. What was her problem?

Herra Aalto returned, carrying Mo's suitcase. "Come. I'll show you to the room you'll share with Kirsti. You two have your own WC and shower. I'm sure you'll find it quite suitable."

He escorted Mo down the hallway and opened the door grandly to reveal a large bedroom with matching twin beds. A birchwood desk in the center of the room bore a very expensive-looking computer, virtual snowflakes drifting across the monitor. Kirsti lay on the bed against the far wall, thumbing through a magazine. She didn't even look up.

"Well, I'll leave you girls to get acquainted." Herra Aalto bowed with a flourish. *"Hyvää yötä."*

"Good night," Mo replied.

Kirsti waited until the door closed. "Nice socks," she said. With that, she stuck a pair of earbuds into her ears and turned back to her magazine.

Mo pressed her lips together and set about unpacking her suitcase. Okay, so her Finland debut wasn't what she had imagined. Her time was totally scheduled, she'd made a fool out of herself with her host family, and her roommate was as icy as the winter night. She wasn't going to let it get her down, though. She'd just have to make sure tomorrow was better.

If only she knew how to do that.

Chapter Two

Mo lay in bed, staring at the shadowed ceiling. Her body ached, she was so tired. Not the good kind of tired like after a hard workout, but the up-all-night-studying-for-finals, waiting-for-a-guy-who-never-calls, chase-around-the-mall-for-jeans-that-fit-and-never-find-them kind of tired. What was she thinking when she told Janessa she would call at five? That was two in the morning in Finland. Not smart. But she needed to talk to her best friend, if only to let her know that the adventure had begun.

She closed her eyes and mentally traced the steps that had led her to Finland. It hadn't been easy. There had been days when she thought she would never escape Park City. Not that she didn't love it there. Her heart would always belong to the rocky mountains, quaking aspens and pines, but she felt smothered back home by her family and her name. All she needed was a chance to get away, if only for a little while, so she could show them—and herself—what she could do.

A study abroad program seemed like a good idea. She started dropping by the counselor's office at school, picking up pamphlets and brochures. When she discovered that S.A.S.S.—Students Across the Seven Seas—was sponsoring a program in Lahti, Finland, called the Scholar Athlete Exchange, she could hardly breathe. Lahti! Home of the famous Lahti Ski Games. Some of the best ski jumpers in the world competed there. She applied that day.

It wasn't easy convincing her parents to let her go. Especially her dad. He stomped around for days growling things like, "Why would you want to go all the way to Finland to train when we have one of the best jumping facilities right here in our backyard?" or "What about the Junior Nationals?" or "You should have stuck with a sport with Olympic potential. If *I* was your coach..."

Finally, her mom came to the rescue. "The experience might be good for her," she'd said, and that was that.

Still, they'd made her work for it. She spent every weekend for six months in the office at the ski school to earn the money to pay for her half of the travel costs and tuition.

She took summer classes so she could stay on track in school the semester she was gone. She even gave up her spot in the Park City Ski Club. That one was tough, but she had no doubts it would be worth it.

Across the room, Kirsti sighed and rolled over in bed. Mo snapped out of her semisleep and checked her watch. Only seven minutes to go. Slowly, silently, she pushed back the thick down comforter and settled her bare feet to the floor, easing her weight forward. The bed slats under her mattress shifted and she froze, watching Kirsti's sleeping form through the darkness. Good. Not even a stir. Mo stood and padded to the door, pausing only long enough to snag her backpack from the foot of the bed.

Cool air licked her toes as she crept down the hallway. In the living room, the building's exterior lighting filtered through the sheer curtains on the windows, illuminating the sculpted-glass coffee table and casting eerie shadows throughout the room. She shivered. Her feet felt as if they were encased in the ice the table was supposed to represent. If she hadn't been so worried about waking Kirsti, she would have gone back to the room for her slippers. Instead, she sank onto the couch and tucked her legs beneath herself as she dug through her backpack for the phone. She squinted in the dim light to punch in the numbers.

Nessa answered on the first ring. "Y-ello."

"Hey. It's me."

"Mo! So you really made it!"

"All in one piece."

"And? What's it like? Are there any cute guys? How does it feel?"

Mo smiled and wrapped herself in the familiarity of Nessa's voice. She recounted the flight and the intense cold and managed to laugh about her disastrous debut in the Aalto home.

"Classic."

"Thanks. I try."

"So, when do you hit the hills?"

"The coach said Monday."

"No training for two days?"

Mo hunched her shoulders. She'd never gone for more than a day without some kind of workout for as long as she could remember. Champions don't take holidays, her dad always said. "Maybe I can get the Aaltos to take me by the Sports Center tomorrow. I mean today. Just to get a feel for the place."

"You'll have to tell me all about it. I'm seriously jealous, you know."

"I wish you could have come with me."

Nessa hesitated just a beat too long before answering. "Yeah. Me, too."

Nice try, but Mo knew the score. Best friends or no,

the exchange thing had been Mo's dream, not Nessa's. Besides, the Junior Nationals were coming up and Nessa stood a good chance of placing this year. Not the best time to leave Park City. "Well, I'm going to miss you."

"Me, too. But, hey, you'll just have to have enough adventure for the both of us."

And that's exactly what Mo planned to do.

Despite the lack of sleep, Mo woke Sunday morning ready to start the day fresh—even though Kirsti seemed determined to keep up the cold-shoulder routine. No biggie. Back home Mo shared her room with a sister who was just starting college. She'd become accustomed to mood swings and actually preferred the silence to the alternative. Mo left Kirsti alone with her irritability and found Rouva Aalto in the kitchen.

"Hyvää huomenta."

Rouva Aalto glanced up from arranging sliced cheese and bread on a platter. "Ah, just in time for breakfast. Good morning to you, too."

Mo eyed the plates and glasses lined up on the counter and offered to put them on the table.

"No, no. You sit. I am nearly finished here."

In the dining room, Herra Aalto was already at the table, surrounded by important-looking papers and talking into his cell phone. He quickly ended his call and greeted Mo. "How did you sleep?"

"Great," she lied.

"Excellent, excellent. Can't have your father thinking that we are mistreating you."

Kirsti slogged into the room and set plates and silverware on the table without so much as looking at Mo. Rouva Aalto followed with the food—rye bread, cheese, yogurt, and a bowl of bright red berries.

"Who was it on the phone, Jormo?"

"It's the Nyström account," he grumbled. "Problems with the itinerary. We'll have to go into the office and make the changes."

Rouva Aalto frowned. "Today?"

He nodded, brow creased. "Many apologies, Maureen," he said. "We had not intended to abandon you your first day here, but I'm sure Kirsti would be happy to show you around the town, won't you, my dear?"

Kirsti nodded, expressionless.

"It's okay," Mo said quickly. "We could wait until you're done and—"

"Nonsense. It will give you girls an opportunity to get to know each other."

Kirsti mumbled something in Finnish that Mo couldn't understand, but judging from the look on Herra Aalto's face, it must not have been very nice.

Mo's stomach tightened. It was going to be a long day.

• • •

From firsthand experience, Mo knew what it felt like to have her time commandeered by her family. It made her almost feel sorry for Kirsti—or it would have if Kirsti hadn't been going out of her way to let Mo know how unhappy she was to be stuck with her. Kirsti took her around the city on the bus, hardly speaking except to give a detached description of some of the buildings or scenery.

When they got off the bus to walk around the *tori*—an outdoor market square packed with colorful vendors' wagons and booths—Kirsti ditched Mo altogether. At first Mo didn't even realize Kirsti was gone. It wasn't until she saw some bright yellow mushrooms in one of the vendor stalls and turned to ask Kirsti what they were called in Finnish that she realized Kirsti wasn't there. Mo wandered with the crowd, walking up and down the rows of stalls and displays, but Kirsti had vanished. What's more, Mo was pretty sure that Kirsti had done the disappearing act on purpose.

Nice one. Since Mo didn't know the language and had no idea how to get back to the Aaltos' house, this was probably meant to make her panic. Well, she wasn't going to give Kirsti the satisfaction. She scanned the *tori*. No way did Mo believe Kirsti would risk her parents' wrath by completely abandoning their guest. She was probably in one of the nearby shops, watching. Mo straightened and strolled casually among the vendors, fingering the coarse reindeer pelts and colorful hand-knit mittens and refusing to look around for Kirsti anymore.

When she caught the scent of cooking sausages, Mo forgot Kirsti altogether. Stomach rumbling, she followed her nose to a stand where a man in a fur hat hovered over a grill, tending what looked like long brown hot dogs. Steam hissed and wavered upward, filling the air with a savory tang. Above the stall, a sign read, *makkara*, 2€. Mo quickly dug out her wallet and gestured for one *makkara*.

The man handed her a sausage wrapped in a napkin. The warmth radiated through Mo's gloves, warming her fingers. Her stomach growled again in anticipation.

"You're not going to eat that, are you?"

Mo turned to find Kirsti watching her, arms folded across her chest. She *knew* it.

"Absolutely," Mo said. She took a big bite of the *makkara*. The flavor and texture reminded her of a cross between a frankfurter and a bratwurst—and it was just as delicious as she had anticipated.

"Do you have any idea what's in those things?" Kirsti sniffed.

Mo almost laughed. It was the exact same thing Nessa said whenever Mo ate hot dogs at home. She shrugged. "Whatever it is, it's good. Try some." Mo broke the sausage in half and extended the uneaten portion to Kirsti, who backed away, shaking her head.

Down the street, a clock tower chimed and Mo automatically looked toward the sound. Three-thirty and the sun had already settled on the horizon—a hazy sphere filtering just enough light through the winter clouds to cast long, muted shadows across the icy street. Only the distant lights of the Sports Center cut through the dusk, illuminating the tops of Lahti's ski-jumping hills. Mo nudged Kirsti's arm and pointed toward the stadium. "Can we go see the ski hills?"

"Why? We'll practically be living there after tomorrow."

"Hey, I can go by myself if you don't want to."

Kirsti's scarf muffled her huff. She muttered to herself in Finnish, but led the way to the bus.

They rode only a few stops before reaching the Sports Center. The driver let them off near a snow-packed parking lot in front of the stadium.

Mo turned around, taking in the stadium and arena and the surrounding buildings. She whistled. "Wow. It's huge. Is this all part of the complex?"

"Yes." Kirsti's voice took on the flat, bored tone of a tour guide at the end of a long day. "There you see the hills and the ski museum, here is the stadium, and over there is for hockey..."

Kirsti's voice faded into the background as Mo stared at the ski-jump hills. Even though she knew that both the 90-meter hill and the 120-meter hill were the same regulation size as the ones she was used to in Park City, they somehow looked bigger. Maybe because the hills back home were built against the side of a mountain. These were freestanding. Even the 64-meter hill looked huge.

"Look! Someone's jumping." Without waiting for a response, Mo took off for the observation area. She could hear Kirsti grumbling behind her, but she didn't pay much attention because she was more interested in the group of jumpers who had lined up on the platforms atop the center hill. Mo held her breath. This was it—exactly what she'd been waiting for. Tomorrow she'd get a crack at those hills.

"All right," Kirsti said, "we've seen it. Let's go."

"Wait! Can't we watch them for a little while?"

"It's freezing out here."

"Just one jump, okay?" Mo pointed to where a jumper perched on the start bar, skis aligned in the tracks. Even from their position near the bottom of the hill, Mo could sense the tension in his posture—like a lynx waiting to spring from the shadows. "See, look. He's just about to go."

Kirsti crossed her arms but didn't refuse.

The starter flag waved and the jumper pushed away from the bar, crouching low as he zoomed down the sharp incline at the top of the hill—the inrun. As he reached the end where the ramp flattened out, he sprang up and forward in one fluid movement, like a bird taking flight. The guy made it look easy—ankles cocked, skis in a perfect

V, arms straight to his sides—grace itself in motion. His landing was just as elegant, knees slightly bent, one foot in front of the other in a perfect telemark.

Forgetting herself, Mo punched the air and let out a loud whoop. "Yes! That was awesome! Did you see him fly?" It was a perfect jump if she ever saw one. Over a hundred and twenty points for sure. If this were a competition, judges could award up to sixty points for completing the elements of a perfect jump: control, balance, graceful flight, and proper landing. He aced them all as far as Mo was concerned. And he'd landed a couple of meters beyond the K point—the jury distance for the hill. That would get him another sixty points for reaching the K point plus two points for each additional meter of distance. Amazing. She caught Kirsti's arm. "Who is that? Do you know him?"

Kirsti snorted. "Too well. He goes to my school."

"Oh, really?" Mo watched his lithe form with interest as he bent to unfasten his bindings. That meant for the next ten weeks he went to *her* school, too. Was he part of SAE? Would they be clubmates? She watched appreciatively as he straightened and swung his skis onto broad shoulders. He strode off the outrun hill, his jumpsuit outlining well-defined muscles. "What's his name?"

Kirsti pulled from Mo's grasp. "Leevi Patrin," she said flatly. "He is *romani*—Gypsy blood. You should stay away

from him. He is a…what do you say in America? A loser?"
She curled her lip and turned away as if the sight of him
was just too much for her delicate sensibilities. "Come, we
should go now." She crunched away through the snow.

Mo followed, but not before she stole another glance
at the Gypsy jumper. Avoid him? No way. Not if she had
anything to say about it.

Chapter Three

Mo woke early Monday morning. Her stomach felt like it was filled with helium, and she wasn't sure if it was nerves or excitement. Probably a mixture of both. She pulled on her favorite pair of jeans and the teal sweater Nessa had given her as a going-away present. She'd said that it brought out the color in Mo's auburn hair and hazel eyes. Whatever. It was comfortable, that's all Mo cared about. Facing a new school, she was going to need all the comfort she could get.

She spent extra time on her hair and makeup, even though she usually didn't bother with either back home.

Her usual look was a ponytail and, if she was really ambitious, a touch of mascara and lip gloss.

Of course, the primping didn't do her much good. Reality slapped her in the face as soon as she stepped outside. That, and the subzero temperature. The cold in Finland was like a living, breathing thing, seeking out any exposed skin and licking it with a freezer-burn tongue. Moist. Penetrating. Intense. Seriously unlike the drier Utah brand of cold she was used to. Mo quickly adjusted her scarf up over her face and pulled her knit hat down to her eyebrows. So much for allure. Coverage was in, cute was out.

At least Herra Aalto drove them to school that morning so they wouldn't have to take the bus—or worse, ride bikes. Mo saw several people pedaling along the snowy streets and couldn't help but stare.

"They have snow tires," Herra Aalto explained when she questioned their sanity. "The tires have little metal studs to help with the traction. Of course, those don't help against the cold, or if one comes across a patch of ice."

He pulled to the curb and stopped. "Here you are. The *lukio*. How would you say it? The high school."

Mo peered out the car window at the old reddish-brown brick building with its rows and rows of square white windows. Students in heavy coats and hats hurried in through the large double doors in the front, toting backpacks. She reached for the handle.

"Wait." Herra Aalto laid a hand on her arm, then twisted around and said something in Finnish to Kirsti, who was seated in the back. Kirsti responded with a long-suffering sigh.

"Come on." She threw open her door. "I will show you to your *Suomen kurssi.*"

"Huh?" Mo bobbed her head in thanks to Herra Aalto for the ride and scrambled out of the car after Kirsti. "My what?"

Kirsti rolled her eyes. "The Finland class. That class is in English, so you don't need a student escort. No one is going to meet you to take you around until afterward."

"Oh." Mo shouldered her backpack. "Well, thanks for showing me where it is."

Kirsti gave Mo a quizzical look and then led the way into the building.

Once inside, Mo decided that the school wasn't that much different from her high school in Park City. Outside, the building had seemed imposing and foreign, but the halls inside felt like home. Same nondescript fixtures, same echoing high-ceiling acoustics, same institutional smell of paper, floor wax, and disinfectant. As much as she had been craving a change, the familiarity was soothing.

She followed Kirsti down a crowded hallway, trying not to look all wide-eyed and new.

"*Hei! Hei,* Kirsti!" A girl with purple-hued hair and about ten earrings in each ear rushed toward them. "Is this your guest?" Without waiting for an answer, she turned her green eyes on Mo. "*Terve!* I am Riia Mattila. *Hauska tutustua!* Pleased to meet you." She extended her hand. Mo shook it.

"*Hauska tutustua*," Mo repeated. "I'm Mo."

Riia's face pinched and she consulted a clipboard she held in her hand. "Mo?"

"It's Maureen, but my friends—"

"Ah. Mo-reen. Yes, I see." She turned to Kirsti. "I volunteer in the *Suomen kurssi.* I can show her the class." Kirsti didn't bother trying not to look relieved. She stepped back as Riia took Mo's arm and steered her down the hallway, throwing a wave back at Kirsti. "*Hei-hei.* I promise to take good care."

Riia leaned close to Mo as they walked so that she could be heard over the noise in the hall. "Some many of us from Lahti have volunteer for the introduction class. I am enjoy talking about my country, so this is fun time for me. Also, I see I am translate for you in calculus, but I should warn that my English is maybe not so good. You will tell me if I mess around, yes?" She plowed ahead before Mo could reply. "You will like the class I think, though I am sorry to say language study is first unit and, poor you, Finnish is the most hard language in the world to learn. Even more hard than English. But I can try to help."

"*Kiitos.* Thank you." Mo worked in the reply as Riia paused to take a breath.

"*Ole hyvä*. You are very welcome."

As they entered the classroom, a girl in the back jumped up from her seat and waved. "Maureen! Maureen Clark!"

Mo's face fell. It was one of the girls from the juniors' ski-jump competition circuit in the States. It stood to reason that there would be people she knew in the program since it was a pretty tight-knit sport, but Mo was disappointed just the same to be recognized immediately. Everyone back home knew her as "One of the Clarks." She'd hoped to be known as herself for once.

The girl pushed her way past a row of desks and hurried over to where Mo was standing. "Oh. My. Gosh. I didn't know you were doing this. That is so cool."

Before the conversation could go any further, the teacher, Herra Kolehmainen, walked into the room and everyone quickly took their seats.

"You would like we sit with her?" Riia asked.

Mo shook her head. "No, that's okay." She glanced over to where the girl was joining her friends—more girls Mo recognized from the circuit. They whispered in a huddle and soon all four girls looked up and waved. Mo forced a smile and waved back. "Let's sit over here." She pointed to a couple of chairs deep in the guys' territory.

"Yes!" Riia giggled. "Good idea."

Mo's selection actually had nothing to do with the guys, although a couple of them were pretty cute. It's just that she had never been comfortable in group situations and she didn't want to feel obligated to make small talk with the girls. Call it a defense mechanism. Sooner or later all conversations drifted to her dad or her family, and if that was the case, she'd rather not have them at all.

As the students took their seats, Mo let her eyes wander around the room. Most everyone she recognized was from the States or Canada, with the exception of three petite Japanese girls who clustered together and giggled behind their hands a lot. Mo watched them as they took their seats. They might look young and shy, but she knew from experience that the Japanese took their jumping very seriously. Those three would probably be her toughest competition.

The girls easily outnumbered the guys, which figured. The women's ski-jump exhibition that SAE had arranged to coincide with the Lahti Ski Games was a pretty big deal for girls. That last vote by the International Olympic Committee, excluding a women's event from the 2010 Olympics, had been a huge blow to the sport. Mo even had clubmates in Park City who had quit jumping to move on to other disciplines. The number of opportunities for women jumpers to compete on the same level with the guys just wasn't there.

That's why the girls' SAE exhibition was so attractive. Historically, only men had been allowed to jump in the Lahti Ski Games, but the top three female competitors in the exhibition would get the nod. They would be allowed

to jump in the games—albeit only as forerunners to check the hill conditions for the male competitors.

That was draw enough for Mo, though. Not since Anita Wold in 1975 had a woman jumped in an exhibition at the games. Mo wanted her name to go down in history, too, not as Kip Clark's daughter, but as one of the women who broke through the gender barrier at the Lahti Ski Games. Eventually women would be able to participate as actual competitors. One by one the obstacles were falling. The Federation of Skiing had voted to include women jumpers in world championship-level competition and Lahti wanted to host the World Cup in a few years, which meant their lineup would include dozens of women. But for now, Mo's group would be groundbreakers.

The bell rang and class began. The teacher, Herra Kolehmainen, didn't waste time on preliminaries but rushed right into the lesson. It didn't take Mo long to realize that Riia had been right about the language. Just the introductory chapter set Mo's head spinning. Forget vocabulary—the pronunciation alone was going to do her in. Even though Riia patiently repeated words for her, Mo could still not hear the difference between a single or a double vowel, or between a *y* or the *o* with the little umlaut over it. And what was up with all the long words? She could swear she saw one in the book with about fifty letters. Like she'd ever be able to say that one!

Riia kept trying to make Mo hold her mouth a certain

way so that she could make the sounds of the letters, but Mo just wasn't getting it. She was relieved when the bell rang and Riia hustled her to the next class.

"Now I must give you to your escort," she said, scanning the crowded hallway. "There he is!"

Mo was pleased to see Riia pointing to a tall blond guy with impossibly blue eyes and a killer smile, who nodded in greeting as they approached.

Riia made the introductions. "Tapio, here is Mo-reen Clark. Mo-reen, here is Tapio Myllymäki. She will take you to computer science."

Mo raised her brows and glanced up at Tapio, who was most definitely not a she.

"She meant to say 'he,'" Tapio said smoothly, managing to give both Riia and Mo a smile that seemed to be directed to each one exclusively. "We do not have a gender-specific pronoun in Finnish," he explained, "so English can be confusing at times."

Riia's hand flew to her mouth. "Oh. I said wrong?"

"Ei se mitään," Tapio gave her a wink. "It's nothing. I'm quite secure with my orientation."

Riia blushed. "Oh. You...I...I must go to class." She retreated, but called back to Mo, "I see you in precalc."

Tapio eyed Mo and tsked. "Calculus? What kind of class is that for a beautiful girl like you?"

Mo mimed sticking her finger down her throat. "Oh, I'm sorry," she said. "Sexist remarks always make me ill."

He grinned. "I'm not sexist. I'm charming."

"Hmmph." Still, she smiled back. "So what's wrong with calculus? Girls with brains intimidate you?"

His smile broadened. "Wouldn't know. Never seen any."

"Perhaps you should try looking above the neckline."

Tapio laughed. "You, I like." He draped an arm around her shoulder. Mo brushed it off like it was dandruff, which made him laugh again. He gave her an exaggerated bow. "Come, I'll show you to class."

He ushered Mo down the hall and into a large room cluttered with desks, computers, and students. The teacher was nowhere to be seen.

"This is the number one best class," Tapio said. "Very easy. Herra Mäki doesn't much care what you do in here so long as you complete the assignments on time. I usually run code or download playlists."

"You think he'd mind if I checked my e-mails?"

"You can do whatever you want. But first come meet the group."

He led her to the back of the room, where he introduced her around to his friends. Not surprisingly, most of them were girls. They welcomed her and tried to include her in their conversation, but they kept slipping into Finnish and Mo couldn't follow what they were saying. She wandered away and poked around at one of the computers.

Unfortunately, a password was required to get onto the Internet and she didn't want to pull Tapio away from his

friends to find out what it was. She found some game pro-
grams and spent most of the class playing freecell.

The teacher finally put in an appearance—during the
last ten minutes of class. The man only hung around long
enough to take attendance and write the assignment on
the whiteboard at the front of the room, then vanished
again.

Tapio dropped into the chair next to Mo. "Here," he
said, pulling a pen from behind his ear and reaching for
her notebook, "I'll translate the assignment for you."

She glanced up from the cards on her screen. "Hmm?
Oh, thanks." She paused. "So, your friends seem nice."

"Yeah, I guess."

"That's real enthusiastic."

He put down the pen. "Well, you know how it is with
the nonskiing types. They know that you compete and they
think it's great, but they don't really get what that means."

Mo nodded. She knew that all too well. Outside her
ski club, only a handful of friends had any clue about the
level of dedication that competition required. On the day
she found out women jumpers had been excluded from
the Olympics yet again, Mo had spent the entire morning
in the bathroom at school, crying. Only her skiing friends
could relate.

"What I really need"—Tapio waggled his brows—"is a
girl who understands me."

Mo laughed. "Good luck with that. Meanwhile, could

you tell me how to log on to the Internet? I was supposed to send my mom and dad a note as soon as I got settled and I haven't done it yet."

"You haven't gotten settled?"

"I haven't written to them."

"Oh." He grinned. "I thought perhaps you found Finland unsettling." Without waiting for a reply, he leaned close to Mo, clacking out the commands on her computer. He smelled of strong soap and even stronger breath. What had he eaten for breakfast? Garlic? She turned her head, trying not to breathe.

"…how you thought it would be?"

"I'm sorry. What?"

He straightened. "Yes, I know my proximity is distracting, but you must try to concentrate."

"Ha."

"I was asking if Finland lives up to your expectations."

"Oh. Sure. I didn't really know what to expect, but I like what I've seen so far."

"I thought so. You are taken with me."

She rolled her eyes.

He grinned. "So no problems? No culture shock?"

"Not really. I feel pretty comfortable here. It helps that so many people speak English."

"Yes, well, we have to study English since we are quite young. As well as Swedish. And another language like French or German or Russian."

"Wow. You speak three languages?"

He squared his shoulders. "Four, actually."

Mo was genuinely impressed. The only language study she'd done was two halfhearted years of Spanish and that was only to fulfill her school's requirement. "Why so many?"

Tapio shrugged "Well, Sweden once occupied our land and theirs remains the second official language, so we have to learn that."

"Yeah, I wondered why the road signs were written in two languages."

"That would be why. And then there's English, the language of diplomacy. And since we need to communicate with the world and hardly anyone learns our language, we take the responsibility to learn more. Knowledge is power, you know."

"I'll be sure to remember that." The bell rang. Mo sighed. "So much for the e-mail."

"I think your parents will live." He held out his hand. "Come on, I'll walk you to your next class. Who do you have?"

Mo ignored his hand and fished her schedule from her backpack. "Um . . ." She chewed her lip, trying to decipher the pronunciation. "Hämäläinen?"

Tapio grimaced. "That should be *ä* as in 'ham.' And you have my sympathies."

"That bad, huh?"

"Let's just say that the ease of computer science with Mäki is inversely proportional to the joy of calculus with Hämäläinen."

"Great."

"Don't worry. I'm sure you'll do fine, you being a girl with brains and all." He inclined his head. "Right this way."

Mo paused when she entered the classroom and tried not to look too lost as she scouted the room for Riia. There she was, sitting in the back row, animatedly talking with a couple of other girls from the SAE group. Mo slid her backpack off her shoulder and started to work her way through the crowd toward them.

And then she saw him—a guy in a beat-up black leather biker jacket and jeans whose posture and attitude seemed so completely different from the other guys at the school that Mo had to stop and stare. He had the whole bad-boy thing going on, the way he leaned back in his chair, one leg hooked up over the side of the desk and the other stretched out in front of him. His chin was raised in a challenging way as he scanned the room—almost as if he owned it.

Mo realized too late that his gaze was making its way to where she stood and she was caught staring. Gaping was more like it. His mocha eyes met hers and she quickly looked away, heat rushing to her face. *Relax*, she told herself. *He's just a guy.* She stole another glance at him, now that his attention had shifted to somewhere else. A smile tugged the corner of her lips. Just a guy. Right.

She took a deep breath and approached his desk. *"Moikka,"* she said in her friendliest voice. Hello.

He glanced at her and raised a brow, expression sharpening, challenging.

Her face flushed and she just about lost her nerve. She gestured to the vacant seat to his right. "May I?"

He dropped his foot to the floor and pushed the chair toward her. Not exactly the response she was hoping for, but at least he didn't tell her to get lost.

"Um, *kiitos*," she managed.

With a half shrug and a barely perceptible nod, he gave her one last look before continuing his scan of the room. Mo settled into her chair, continuing her scan of him. All the parts of the component were pleasant enough—hair, chin-length coffee-brown waves partially hidden beneath a Halti knit hat; skin the color of spun honey; nose, straight and narrow; cheekbones, high and wide; jaw, strong. His jacket spanned broad shoulders and his jeans encased long legs. Yeah, great parts, no doubt about it. But it was the whole that got to her. Beneath the bad-boy posture, she sensed something else. A quiet defiance layered with an unmistakable aura of confidence. The combination was irresistible.

She wanted to talk to him, but she had no idea what to say. He hadn't exactly responded to her earlier overture.

The sound of the heavy classroom door slamming shut drew her attention to the front of the room. Well, most of her attention anyway. She did manage to keep Biker Boy within her peripheral vision. He straightened and pulled a tattered notebook from inside his jacket, focused as the teacher took the podium.

"I thought you see me," a voice whispered in her ear. "I was save you a seat."

Mo twisted around to find Riia slipping into the chair next to her. Guilt prickled. *"Anteeksi,"* she said softly. "I'm sorry. I..." Her voice trailed off. What could she say? I wanted to hit on this guy? With an apologetic smile, she opened her calculus book and tried her best to concentrate on the lesson. Her thoughts kept slipping back to the Biker Boy, though, and she spent more class time trying to think of something clever to say to him than she did trying to understand functions and derivatives.

She tore a piece of paper from her notebook and scribbled a note to Riia.

This guy sitting next to me—what is his name?

Riia read the message and glanced quickly at Herra Hämäläinen before bending over the paper, pen scratching furiously. Mo's mouth dropped open when she read the answer. Biker Boy was none other than the Gypsy jumper, Leevi Patrin.

She stole another glance at him, remembering Kirsti's pronouncement that he was a loser. She quickly sifted through all the things Kirsti had done and said over the past two days. How many of them had been in Mo's best interest? Maybe this was one situation in which Mo would have to find out the truth for herself.

Chapter Four

Mo's breath froze in miniature clouds as she left Kirsti in the stadium dressing room and stepped out into the afternoon air. It had begun to snow, small powdered-sugar snowflakes that dusted everything in white.

She turned slowly, taking in the feel of standing on the field of the Lahti stadium. To her right, the ski jumps stretched up into the low-hanging clouds, the lights in soft focus through the fog. Oh, how she wanted to climb up on those hills! It wouldn't be today. Coach Peltonen had said something about working into it. Today they were to do cardio. At least they'd be skiing, though. Cross-country.

Good thing Mo had come prepared. She'd brought both her wide, long skis for jumping and the thinner, more proportionate cross-country skis.

"Maureen!" Mo turned to see the girl from Finland class break away from her friends and come walking toward her.

"Hi. How's it going?"

"Great! How about you? How'd you do in school?"

"Good. It was a little hard to understand in math, though," Mo admitted.

"I know! I had chemistry, and I swear, if we weren't learning the elements in Latin, I'd have been totally lost."

"So." Mo's brain spun, trying to think of something to say. She was no good at small talk. "Is it cold enough for you?" Well, there was a clichéd conversation starter.

"Nah. I'm from Michigan—a UPER, you know, from the Upper Peninsula. Half of my neighbors are Finnish-Americans who come back *here* to warm—" She stopped and grabbed Mo's arm. "Don't look now, but hot guy alert."

Mo glanced over her shoulder and smiled. *"Hei,* Tapio."

He strode toward them. "Ladies."

The girl turned up the high beams on her smile. *"Hei."*

Mo left them to their flirting ritual and ran through a series of warm-up exercises on her own until the girl returned to her group and Tapio came to stand by Mo.

"You ready for this?" he asked.

"I'm always ready."

He shook his head. "Peltonen runs us hard."

"And what? I look frail to you? You don't think I can handle it?"

He laughed and backed away. "Without a doubt. I'll be keeping my eye on you."

Mo opened her mouth, ready for a comeback, when she noticed a familiar figure crossing the snowy field with Coach Peltonen. He was dressed now in Gore-Tex and Lycra instead of denim and leather, but there was no mistaking his build or the aggressive set of his chin. The words she had meant to say stuck in her throat. "Ahm…" she garbled.

Tapio grinned. "I leave you speechless, yes?"

"Speechless," Mo agreed, eyes on Leevi Patrin.

Coach Peltonen gathered the group of athletes. "We're going for distance this afternoon, not necessarily for speed. Remember to pace yourself so we don't see any injuries. We have a big week ahead of us."

Mo slid a look at Tapio. "Looks like you're off the hook. If it had been a race, I might have had to bury you."

He gave her half a laugh, but there was no mistaking the competitive edge to his smile.

"The course is twenty kilometers," Coach Peltonen said. "Patrin here knows the route. Follow him."

Brows raised, Mo whispered to Tapio, "What is he, Coach's favorite or something?"

Tapio frowned. "Hardly."

Before Mo could ask what he meant, Tapio hurried off to get his skis.

Despite the coach's caveat, their cardio run turned out to be very much about speed. In fact, it was like a race from beginning to end.

Leevi led the pack, of course. Mo knew instinctively that she shouldn't have been surprised at that. He seemed like the kind of guy who had something to prove. Tapio tried to keep up with Leevi, which meant that Mo had to kick up her pace as well; she wasn't about to let Tapio totally smoke her. Mo caught glimpses of Kirsti as she tried to pull ahead, and then lost her when she fell behind. Not by far, though. Mo could hear her rasping breath and grunts of effort not more than a ski length away.

As the group glided across a snowy field, Mo couldn't help but admire Leevi's relaxed posture, the ease in his stride. The more she tried not to notice, the more acutely aware she was of him.

Leevi's route wound past trees and fences draped in gingerbread snow, through long stretches of stark white fields, up and down rolling hills, and finally back to where they started. Mo hadn't even realized how long they'd been at it until the stadium came into view. Twenty kilometers, and she'd never slowed once. As the knowledge sank in, Mo began to feel the burn. Still, she pushed herself to the

finish line before she allowed herself to ease off, taking a lap around the stadium field to bring her heart rate down. Near the stadium tunnel that led to the locker rooms, she slid to a stop. Hands on knees, she sucked in lungfuls of frozen air, moisture freezing on her scarf as she let it out again. She didn't even notice Leevi until he'd skied up beside her.

He extended his hand. "Nice run," he said.

She blinked. "Oh. Uh, thanks." Straightening, she tucked her poles under one arm and shook his hand, too taken aback by his civility to think of anything else to do. He nodded, and skied off.

Mo blinked after him, at once pleased and confused. She bent and undid her bindings, smiling to herself. That is, until she straightened and saw Kirsti watching from the tunnel, arms folded tightly across her chest. Mo dipped her head in greeting and shouldered her skis.

"Great practice, huh?" She clomped through the tunnel in her ski shoes, leaving Kirsti to scowl alone.

That night after dinner, Rouva Aalto rose to clear the dishes. "You girls are certainly quiet this evening."

"Worn out from practice, eh?" Herra Aalto folded his newspaper he had been reading. "What you need is a proper Finnish sauna. We do have the room scheduled this evening. Would you like to use it?"

It took Mo a second to realize what he was talking

about because he had pronounced the word "sow-nah."

"Oh. Yes, that sounds nice."

Kirsti coughed. "I don't know, *Iskä*. It might make her feel uncomfortable."

Mo stiffened at the condescension in Kirsti's tone. "Why do you say that?"

"Because you Americans are so prudish about getting naked." She looked to her father. "Do you remember those *ääliöt* in the last tour group who insisted on taking sauna wearing their bathing suits?"

Mo had no idea what allie-whatever meant, but it didn't sound complimentary. She forced a laugh. "Swimsuits? You're kidding." Of course, Kirsti never had to know that Mo had packed her own swimsuit after reading in her brochure about Finnish saunas—somehow missing the part about doing it in the buff. She forced a smile. "I'm up for it."

"Wonderful." Herra Aalto leaned back in his chair. "Of course, we'll let you girls have the room to yourself. And then one of these weekends we'll take you out to the möki so you can do *avanto*. Now that's the proper way to take sauna."

Mo frowned. *"Avanto?"*

"Oh, yes. You must try the authentic experience. Sauna is an important part of the Finnish lifestyle, you understand. It's ingrained in our culture. Most every home or apartment building has a sauna. Sauna baths cleanse

both our bodies and our spirits. Even in wartime, soldiers built portable saunas in their camps. It's that much a part of our lives."

Rouva Aalto cleared her throat. "Jormo, please. I'm sure Maureen does not need a cultural lesson."

"No, it's okay," Mo said. She actually found this kind of stuff fascinating. "What was that other thing you were talking about? The murky?"

Herra Aalto laughed. "A *möki* is a lake house. Most everyone either has one or has access to one. As you may have noticed, there's no shortage of lakes in Finland! And *avanto*…" He rubbed his hands together. "*Avanto* you must experience for yourself."

"Great," Mo said. "Let's do it. Uh, what is it?"

He smiled his salesman smile. "Don't worry. You shall find out when the time is right."

Kirsti pushed away from the table. "I'm going to go down now."

"Great." Mo stood. "Lead the way."

The "sauna room" was actually broken up into three rooms—a cloakroom–size area lined with wooden benches and hooks on the wall, a shower room, and the sauna itself. Following Kirsti's lead, Mo undressed in the first area and showered off in the second. There were no partitions in the changing room or in the showers, but this was nothing new to Mo. She'd had to share locker rooms before, and with six siblings, she was used to having no privacy. A little nudity was not going to freak her out.

Kirsti handed Mo a small towel. "For sitting on," she said. Two larger towels hung on hooks by the door.

The smell of damp cedar surrounded Mo as she stepped into the heat of the sauna. Double tiers of deep, wooden benches lined the walls on two sides of the room. Mo laid down her towel and sat on the nearest bench, heat settling over her like a damp blanket.

Kirsti stood near the door next to a wall-mounted heating unit—brushed chrome with a wire enclosure on top that held a jumble of black rocks. Kirsti read the attached thermostat. "Only seventy-nine," she muttered, and adjusted the temperature upward.

Mo mentally calculated Celsius into Fahrenheit. A hundred and seventy-four degrees seemed plenty hot to her, but she wasn't about to say anything to Kirsti and be branded a wuss.

On the bench near the heating unit sat a bucket of water and a ladle. Kirsti took the ladle and threw water onto the rocks. It hissed and spit and sent a wave of steam rolling through the room like a superheated thunderstorm.

"This is called *löyly*." Kirsti tossed another ladleful of water on the rocks and gave Mo a sidelong glance. "The steam makes it feel hotter, though it isn't really. If it gets to be too much for you, let me know." She added more water. "Most Americans can never last the entire hour."

Mo narrowed her eyes. Subtle. She blinked away a bead of sweat and forced a smile. "No, this is great."

"Yes, but if you really want to feel it, you should sit on the top bench. Heat rises, you know."

Mo climbed up to the top bench. "Oh, yeah. Much better." She drummed her fingers. "Now what?"

Kirsti cocked her head. "You sweat." She threw more *löyly* onto the rocks. "To rid your body of impurities."

She wasn't kidding about the sweat. Before long Mo couldn't tell if the water beading on her skin was perspiration or condensation from the steam, but it didn't matter. Either way, she was dripping. And hot. Very hot. She began to feel dizzy, but she wasn't about to cave. She leaned back against the wall and closed her eyes.

"Now the *vihta.*" Kirsti's voice sounded far away.

Mo forced one eye open. "The what?"

Kirsti pointed to what looked like a bundle of sticks soaking in a bucket of water near the door. "The birch branches."

Mo pushed away from the wall and climbed unsteadily down to pull one of the bundles out of the bucket. Water dripped from its curled gray-green leaves. "What's it for?"

"To hit yourself."

Right. What did she look like, an idiot? "No, really."

"Really." Kirsti reached for the bundle. "I'll show you." She took the branches and slapped her back, legs and arms until her pale skin blushed pink. "*Vihta* helps the circulation."

Unsure, Mo picked up another bundle of branches and whacked it against her thigh. The skin smarted and tingled and she drew in a hiss of hot air. Kirsti laughed.

Mo ground her teeth. Real funny. She slapped the switch against herself again, more softly this time. Once she got the hang of it, she had to admit it actually felt good.

Throwing aside her *vihta*, Kirsti stood and headed toward the door.

Mo fought a grin. She'd done it. She'd outlasted Kirsti. "Done already?"

Kirsti hmmphed. "Not even close. I'm going to roll in the snow."

"Um, what?"

"Roll. In. The. Snow." She exited the sauna without looking back.

Mo didn't believe for one minute that Kirsti was serious, but there had been a challenge in the other girl's voice and Mo wasn't about to let that pass.

She came out of the sauna just in time to see Kirsti pull open the heavy metal door that led outside. A blast of frigid air rushed into the room.

Nice bluff, Mo thought. Like Kirsti was really going to go out there in the open, naked, where everyone could see.

But then ... she did!

Mo stood gaping. Was she crazy? Or was this another challenge? Well, if Kirsti could do it, Mo could, too.

Taking a deep breath, she bolted out the door and dove into the nearest snowbank. The cold swarmed over her like icy, biting ants. She shrieked and rolled like a Labrador, jumped up, and ran back inside.

"That was insane!" She started brushing off the snow—until she saw that Kirsti was letting it cling to her skin as she walked calmly back to the sauna.

Mo let her hand drop and suppressed a shiver as she followed Kirsti yet again. In the sauna, she climbed up to the top bench and sat on her towel, trying not to flinch as a clump of snow slid down her back.

"This is great," she said, teeth chattering.

It didn't take long to feel the heat of the sauna, though. More snow melted and slithered downward, trailing icy rivulets. Mo shivered and sweated, at once hot and frozen. Her nerves tingled. It was the strangest thing she had ever experienced. And she couldn't wait to do it again.

For the entire hour, Mo and Kirsti each tried to outlast, outsweat, and outtough the other. They cranked the heat to ninety degrees Celsius, threw *löyly* on the stones until the sauna became a steam bath, whacked themselves with the birch branches until their skin glowed sunburn red, and ran in and out of the snow three more times.

They might have kept going, too, except that just as Mo ran outside the last time, headlights from a car pulling into the parking lot lit the snow ahead of her. She shrieked and dropped to the ground, the light sweeping over her prone and freezing figure like in one of those old World War II movies.

"Inside! Inside!" Kirsti urged. Mo pushed herself up and ran in a crouch back to the open door. The two raced for the sauna and collapsed onto the benches, laughing.

Kirsti wiped tears from her eyes. "You should have seen your face!"

"My face? I was worried about the rest of me!"

"At least you could come inside. I got locked out one time."

"No way."

"Yes. With my mother. The door closed behind us and we had to tap on the neighbor's window so he would go open it."

"I would have died."

Kirsti laughed. "I wanted to. And there stood my mother, all businesslike and proper…"

Mo laughed even harder, imagining her own mom standing naked in the bushes near their neighbors' window, trying to maintain her dignity.

They rode the elevator back up to the apartment in silence. Mo couldn't have been more relaxed; her muscles

felt as if they had melted along with the snow. Even better, she got the feeling that by sticking it out in the sauna, she had crossed some sort of threshold with Kirsti.

She brushed her teeth and put on her pajamas in a sort of contented stupor—until she looked up and noticed Kirsti sitting on her bed across the room, watching her. She wasn't smiling. Mo stilled. "You okay?"

Kirsti shrugged. She dropped her gaze and studied her hands for a moment. Finally she spoke. "My father is a big fan of your father," she began slowly. "When he arranged for you to stay with us, that was all he could talk about. For months it was Kip Clark this and Maureen Clark that. I was sure you would be a spoiled American who thought she was better than everyone else."

Uncertainty coiled in Mo's stomach. She smiled shakily, trying to keep the mood light. "Yeah? Well, I pretty much decided you were a pampered princess who would never in a million years apologize for anything."

Kirsti glanced up. "Who said I was apologizing?" She half smiled. "And what do you mean, pampered?"

"Oh, come on. Your mom and dad—"

"Believe me; everything they do is for their business. I'm not pampered, I'm an investment." She laughed, but Mo could tell she wasn't joking.

They sat quietly for a moment, but Mo imagined a thread of understanding stretching between them. She knew what it was like to feel that she was just a part of her parents' image. Everything she did had to reflect well on her dad's precious ski school. He had not been pleased when Mo decided to take up ski jumping because, besides that whole "it will never get you to the Olympics" thing, it meant that she would be training at the Olympic Park instead of at his facility, and how would that look to people?

She considered telling Kirsti about that, but hesitated. It might be a little too personal. She searched for something more neutral to say. "Your mom and dad seem proud of you."

Kirsti shrugged. "If I win. They are not much interested otherwise."

"I wish my dad was like that. Not so interested, I mean. He doesn't think I can do anything on my own. I thought he'd be a little less involved when he wasn't my coach anymore, but then he just started giving my jump coach pointers."

"He didn't."

"I swear. He still does. I want to crawl into a hole whenever he shows up at the park. Sometimes I just want him to leave me alone."

"Varo mitä toivot—se voi toteutua," Kirsti murmured.

"What does that mean?"

"Be careful what you wish for. It might come true."

They fell silent again and Mo felt like she had just killed the conversation. She fished for another angle. "So how did you get involved with the SAE?"

A cloud passed over Kirsti's face. She lowered her voice. "Our company is the sponsor."

"Wait. We have a *sponsor*?"

Kirsti nodded and picked at her comforter. "Our travel company pays for that trip to Kemi at the end of the term. In return, the SAE books all their future travel arrangements through us."

"Whoa."

"Yes, but not many in the group know, so please do not talk of it. People already think I get special treatment because Coach Peltonen is a friend of the family."

"Yeah, I know how that feels."

Kirsti nodded. "I suppose you do."

When they turned off the lights, Mo snuggled down into her blankets with a sigh. She wasn't naïve enough to think that she and Kirsti would wake up in the morning and suddenly be best friends. But they were beginning to understand each other, and that was a start.

Chapter Five

Mo stood in the middle of the gymnasium, catching her breath. She was tired, she was sweaty, and she wanted to do what she'd come for. Jump! All week long, Coach Peltonen had had the group Nordic skiing, lifting weights, running the track, and even playing volleyball. Okay, that last one was kind of fun, and helped develop their jumping skills, but so far they hadn't so much as looked at the hills, let alone jump them.

When were they going to fly?

Riia nudged Mo. "One more."

Mo snapped back to the task at hand, which at the

moment was diagonal leg bounds. She hated diagonal leg bounds. She made a pathetic face at Riia, who had ended up as Mo's partner for the afternoon. Everyone had to have a partner as they rotated through a circuit of aerobic, resistance, and plyometric exercises.

Riia smiled sympathetically, but she didn't budge. "One more time."

"I'll race you."

The smile broadened. At her signal, she and Mo bounded down the length of the floor mat like a couple of off-balance kangaroos, zigzagging from one foot to the other. Mo was ahead; she would have won, too, if Riia hadn't suddenly crashed to the mat, bringing Mo down with her.

"Hey, no cheat—" Mo stopped when she saw Riia's face. "Are you okay?"

Riia sat on the mat, holding her ankle. "It is nothing." She tried to laugh it off, but pain pinched her smile. Coach Peltonen blew his whistle and it was time to change stations. Riia's smile, shaky though it was, abruptly vanished.

Mo helped Riia to her feet. "Maybe you should sit this round out."

"It is only a twisting. You need a partner to—"

Mo shook her head. "I'm good. Go on."

Riia frowned, but limped obediently over to the side. Mo moved on to the double box jump, which she hated even more than diagonal leg bounds. It consisted of jumping off a ten-inch box and then springing back up onto a thirty-six-inch box. Not fun, but it was meant to develop the muscles that would give her good distance when she jumped, so she wasn't going to slack off, either.

She'd done two reps and jumped off the small box for a third when a voice broke her concentration. "Coach said you needed a spotter."

Startled, Mo didn't quite get the height she needed for the large box and smacked her shins against the edge. She hissed in a breath. Strong arms caught her as she fell.

Leevi set her unceremoniously back on her feet. "We'll need to get you some shin guards if you're going to jump like that."

Mo looked up into his dark brown eyes and her mouth went dry. "Well, I was just...you know...that was..." she garbled.

He raised a brow, and she felt herself shrinking inward. Great. The first time she has a chance to really talk to him and she turns into a babbling fool.

"Try it again," he said.

Feeling like a total idiot, Mo did the exercise again, jumping down from the small box and back up onto the large one. Unfortunately, she was so nervous with him standing there watching that she landed off balance and had to windmill her arms to keep from falling off.

"Try to land with both feet at once," he said. Like that wasn't what she had been trying to do.

Mo repeated the exercise three more times. He watched

her wordlessly, nodding when she got her form right, shaking his head when she was a little off. Her face burned hotter with every jump until she couldn't decide which smarted worse—her shins or her pride.

Finally, Coach Peltonen blew his whistle to end the circuit and called for all the athletes to come together.

Mo stepped down from the box. "Um, thanks for spotting."

He gave her one of those "yeah, whatever" cool-guy nods, but his eyes held hers steadily. Then he turned and walked away. Mo stared after him, all sorts of tingly sensations pinging around inside like a pinball machine.

The coach blew his whistle again. "You now have a twenty-minute break," he called. "Get changed and prepare your equipment. We'll be coming off the K64 today to see where you stand."

"Finally," Riia muttered, "I thought we never get to jump."

Mo eyed Riia's ankle. "Will you be okay jumping?"

Riia pressed her lips together. "I make myself okay."

Mo zipped up her jumpsuit. She hated the way it fit—snug enough to meet International Ski Federation regulations, but saggy enough to make her backside look big. Of course, it had been fitted and refitted before she came. If there was anything competition judges were strict about, it was the fit of the suit. A loose suit that could give extra

lift or distance was considered unfair and would be disqualified. At least the things were just as unflattering on
everyone else.

Kirsti stuck her head in the dressing room. "Did you
wax your skis yet?"

"Yeah."

"What color did you use?"

Mo thought for a minute. "Blue." Each color of ski wax
was specially formulated for different temperatures and
conditions. The lower the temperature, the harder the
wax.

"It's getting colder. Better use the green."

Mo sighed and grabbed her helmet and goggles. Break
was almost over. She didn't have much time.

When Mo entered the wax room, Riia was bent over her
skis, running a wax iron over the bottoms. "*Hei.* I thought
you do yours already."

"Kirsti said I should use the green."

"Yes. It become cold once the sun go down."

Mo fastened her ski in the grip and started dripping
melted wax on the surface. "I can't wait for this!"

Riia looked up. "You will wait." She ran a plastic scraper
down the length of her ski. "Boys go first."

Mo glanced up. "We don't go together?"

"Ha. Many men do not see the jump as a woman sport.
For them, we will always follow the man."

Wasn't *that* the truth. Even in the United States, where

the women's team was well established, men consistently got more sponsorship, more media coverage, and more prize money. And *they* had been able to jump in the Olympics for over eighty years.

"Could be worse," Mo said. "At least we get to jump the same hill."

"Ah, yes. For that we must be grateful."

Sure enough, when they got outside it was the guys Coach Peltonen first called to the top of the hill. Riia pursed her lips and shot Mo a "what did I tell you" look. Mo shrugged. "Coach is saving the best for last, that's all."

Tapio swaggered past them. "I've got first run. Watch and learn, ladies. Watch and learn."

Mo exchanged a look with Riia and they burst out laughing. Mo's smile froze, though, as Leevi neared. She tried to act casual as he walked by, but she couldn't help staring.

As if he could read her thoughts, Leevi turned to look at her. He met her eye and nodded. She quickly turned away, feeling obvious and awkward. Her face burned in spite of the cold. What was it with him? Whenever she got near him, she lost all connection with her brain cells.

Well, okay; the guy was seriously hot. And when he jumped? Watch out. But she'd had good-looking club-mates before and they'd never affected her this way. She leaned against her skis and watched Leevi climb the long stairs to the top of the hill, then joined the other girls along the fence to watch the guys jump. Leevi jumped dead last. And as she expected, his jumps were magic.

The guys made three runs each, and then, at long last, the girls were called up. Mo could hardly contain her excitement. Finally! This is what she had been waiting for.

When her turn came, she slid onto the start bar, anticipation buzzing up and down her spine. She pulled her goggles into place, looking from the line of her skis to the track and the steep incline of the inrun. Everything switched to slow motion as she waited for the green light, barely breathing.

When the signal came, she leaned into her crouch and pushed away from the bar, centering her weight over her skis. She raced down the inrun, muscles coiled for the take-off as the platform rushed forward to meet her. When the end of the ramp came into view, she sprang up and out.

Time suspended altogether as she hung in the air. Floating. Flying. She wanted to laugh, to shout. Even when she landed a full ten meters short of the last jumper. Whatever. She could work on that. But she'd done it! Her first jump in Finland!

The excitement carried her through the next jump, but by the third she realized that compared to everyone else, her jumping fell short. Literally. And that didn't seem right. She'd jumped against most of the girls before on the circuit, and while she hadn't always been on top, she'd never been at the bottom, either.

One thing was certain. If she had any chance of finishing in the top three and jumping in the games, she was going to have to do something about her distance.

Mo sat in her computer science class, staring at the blinking cursor. She had been in Finland over a week and still hadn't written her parents a letter, even though they had e-mailed her every other day and had even called the Aaltos to check on her. It was just too hard to think of anything to say. "Having a great time, glad you're not here" didn't have the right ring to it. She sighed, set her fingers on the keyboard and sat for a long while before she could think of anything to write.

TO: kclark@email.com
FROM: mntmojo@email.com
SUBJECT: Weekly Report

Hi, Mom and Dad,

Got your message on my cell and Mrs. Aalto said you called the house while I was gone. Sorry I missed you. I do keep the cell with me, Dad, but we aren't allowed to have phones on during school hours and of course I leave it in the locker room at practice.

Sorry it's taken me so long to write. You would not believe how busy they keep us! Between practice and school, there's hardly any downtime. We're already speaking some Finnish in my overview class, but it's not easy. I learned to ask where the post office is (*Anteeksi, tiedättekö missä on lähin posti?*)—even though I might not understand the reply. Are you proud or what?

The Aaltos are nice. Their travel company is doing a lot of business so they're really busy. Plus Rouva Aalto is like a Finnish Martha Stewart and she loves to cook and throw big parties. They had one (a party, that is) for some clients last night and we had a lot of traditional Finnish food. My favorite was the *karjalan piirakka*. It's kind of a football-shaped rye pastry with rice filling that they eat with egg butter (minced-up hard boiled eggs mixed with butter. I know it sounds gross, but it was really good, I promise.).

Thanks for attaching those pictures to your last e-mail... but please, I beg you, do not show anyone else the one of me in that hideous bridesmaid dress. (And don't tell my new sister-in-law I said that.)

I'm working hard in practice. Coach Peltonen Is great.

Well, I have to go to class. I miss you. Say hi to everyone for me.

Love,

Mo

Once she pressed send, she felt much better. Of course, she would have felt better still if she could have unloaded about how things were *really* going.

Even though she had only three classes, she could tell

that it was going to be hard to keep up in school. She'd thought that the Finland class was going to be cake; just a few facts here and there, maybe taste some Finnish food and listen to some folk music or something. She was wrong. Dead wrong. Not only was the class expected to learn an insane amount of vocabulary each day, but they were supposed to be writing research papers on Finnish history. She knew nothing about Finnish history. Well, sure, that was kinda the point, but Finnish history spanned thousands of years. Too much history, too little time.

Meanwhile, Herra Kolehmainen and Coach Peltonen were taking the exchangees around Lahti after practice to check out such exciting sites as Lake Vesijärvi's frozen harbor, a church designed by some Finnish architect (the name was Aalto, just like Kirsti's, but no relation), and a sculpture park where all the sculptures were buried in snow. Oh, yes. And she was supposed to write about each one of these adventures in her *Suomen päiväkirja*, or Finland diary, for class—an exercise that usually took longer than the outings themselves because she could hardly ever think of anything to say. The result was that she was already behind in the class.

At least the computer science class had been easy so far, which was more than she could say for precalc. She hated that class. It wasn't that Mo didn't like math; she usually did. But it was different here. Professori Hämäläinen's class was *hard*. Or maybe it was just hard to concentrate in there and be aware of Leevi Patrin at the same time.

And she didn't even want to talk about practice.

"Why so melancholy? Pining for me?" Tapio dropped into the chair next to Mo's. He was apparently done making his daily flirtation rounds with the other girls in the class.

Mo switched off the computer. "That's it. How did you know?"

"I have a sixth sense where women are concerned."

"Aha. And right now I am thinking...?"

He gave her an evil grin. "I'm a gentleman. I would never speak such thoughts out loud."

"Wow. That's uncanny."

"It's a gift." He leaned an elbow on the desk. "So, what are you doing after practice tonight?"

The bell rang. "Oops. Gotta run. Can't be late." She grabbed her books and bolted before Tapio could say anything more. That innocent little question sounded a bit too much like a prelude to asking her out or something. Tapio might be cute, but she wasn't feeling any chemistry. Besides, she had a cardinal rule about dating clubmates—don't. She'd seen it happen too many times, clubmates getting involved, the relationship going sour, practices becoming awkward...for everyone in the club. Best to just avoid the whole thing.

• • •

In calculus, Mo grabbed a seat in the back row and set her backpack on the seat next to hers to save a spot for Riia. She'd decided the back row was the place to be. For one thing, it was easier to hide from Professori Hämäläinen back there. Getting called upon to answer a problem was a painful proposition in that class since the *professori* spoke only in Finnish and she could answer only in English and Riia had to do the translating for both. But also, the back row afforded the perfect vantage point to check out people…people like Leevi, who just happened to be walking into the room at that very moment.

Mo pulled out her book and opened it on her desk and tried not to be totally obvious about watching him. Unfortunately, she failed. He glanced up and looked directly at her, nodding in acknowledgment. A hot chill ran through her—kinda like when she was sitting in the sauna with clumps of snow sliding down her back, only much more intense—and she quickly looked away. Then she felt stupid for looking away without nodding back or something, but by then it was too late to give any kind of greeting signal, so she just sat, face burning, and stared at her math book.

Oh, yeah. She was so going to fail this class.

By Friday, Mo could see that calculus wasn't her only problem. All week, the club worked on their jumps, and all week, Mo landed short. The hills felt different than at home. That's what she wanted to tell herself, anyway. How else could she explain the fact that while everyone else seemed to be jumping farther than normal, she wasn't even reaching her personal best? She hung behind after practice to talk to Coach Peltonen.

"You want me to wait for you?" Kirsti asked.

"No," Mo said quickly. "Go on. I'll meet you at home."

She took her time packing up her gear while she waited for the coach to finish his paperwork.

"Miss Clark." He looked surprised. "What can I do for you?"

"I need help with my jumps."

"Well, you are having some style issues, but we've just gotten started. They'll iron out with more practice. I have faith in you."

She blew out a breath. "Thanks. That's what I was hoping. I really think I need more airtime. Maybe I could stay after practices and—"

He shook his head. "I'm sorry, Mo. That won't work. Between our schedule here and the cultural activities, we're stretched too thin as it is. Besides, the Lahti Ski Club will be using the hills in the evenings. We'll have to work on your technique during regular practice."

Mo's shoulders drooped. Regular practice wasn't going to be enough. Somehow, she'd just have to figure out a way to work in more time on her own.

Chapter Six

Saturday's practice went about how Mo had expected it would. Warm-ups, a little cardio work, and then they hit the hills. Of course, Mo finished dead last for distance once again.

"Don't be so worry." Riia cornered Mo as they boarded the van for their afternoon tour of a historical museum. "Many people say these hills can be hard to jump."

Mo pulled off her gloves. "No one else seems to be having a problem."

"Well, at least your form is good."

"Yeah, for a rock."

Riia laughed at that, but she didn't offer any more plati-tudes. Mo stared out the bus window, her breath fogging the glass, and watched the ice-crusted buildings pass by. Washed colorless in the twilight, the city streets looked bleak. Almost as bleak as her prospects for getting past the exhibition.

She knew what her dad would say in this situation; he'd say her mind wasn't in the game. She had to stop letting discouragement and outside distractions keep her from her goal. If she was going to jump in the Lahti Games, she had to bring her stuff to the hills in the exhibition, and "her stuff" seemed to be sorely lacking at the moment.

Before long, the bus lumbered into the parking lot of the old "coach house" bus station. The historical museum, or *historiallinen museo* as it said on the handout, was actu-ally an old mansion located right behind the station. It had been built over a hundred years before, by one of the early settlers of the city. The place was nice enough to look at and everything, but Mo just couldn't get excited about it; her mind—and her heart—was still back on the hills.

Good thing Riia had come along; she kept up a running commentary on what they were seeing, so even though Mo was only half listening, at least she'd have *something* to write in her *Suomen päiväkirja*. On the other hand, glad as she was for the help, Mo still didn't get why Riia had decided to come on the tour. Since the cultural stuff wasn't required for the local athletes, most of them had made a

break for it the minute practice was over. Kirsti left so fast she'd barely even said good-bye. Only Tapio and Riia had chosen to stick around.

"Do you find ideas here?" Riia asked.

"Huh?"

"Ideas. For your paper."

"Oh." Mo shrugged. "I don't know. I really have been giving it a lot of thought, but I just can't decide on a topic. Nothing here really speaks to me."

Riia's brows pinched. She looked to Tapio. "What does this mean, 'speaks to me'?" But Tapio was busy laughing with the girl from Michigan. Riia fell silent and didn't say much else for the rest of the tour.

Finally, Herra Kolehmainen released them. It was after six by then, cold and dark, but Mo didn't feel like going home just yet.

"Hey, Riia, I was thinking of heading back over to the Sports Center. You want to come?"

Riia watched Tapio wander away with Miss Michigan. "Yes. Please."

Under the glare of the stadium lights, they stood and watched the men's club jump from the K120 *suurmäki*— the big hill—until Mo's feet grew numb and her nose felt like a dripping icicle. She dabbed at it with a tissue and turned to Riia. "Is there somewhere we can go to warm up for a little bit?"

"The *hiitomuseo* is open. The ski museum. There is café where has big window so we may watch from inside." Riia pointed to an oblique wood-and-glass building situated between the stadium and the seating area for the ski jumps.

The café was closed, but Mo and Riia were able to stand in the corner and watch through the floor-to-ceiling window. From their new vantage point, they could see from top to base of all three hills as they watched the men jump.

On one side of the outrun at the bottom of the *suurmäki* was a long cement wall embedded in the landing area. "What's that?"

"Oh!" Riia's eyes lit up. "That is for the swim pool. No practice on the suurmäki in the summer. We have the pool just there. Practice continue on the K90 and K64, so one may swim at the pool and the watch ski jumping at the same time."

Mo laughed, imagining how surreal that must be.

"For the games," Riia continued, "the opposite is true. Only *suurmäki* is jumped. In front of the other hills, people fill the whole area to watch."

Mo pressed her nose against the cold glass, fixated on the hill. If only she could get her jumps right, it would be her coming down the *suurmäki* in the games. She'd learned the physics of it way back in grade school. Now she had to make it happen.

In fifth grade, as one of Park City's top-ranked alpine skiers in her dad's youth farm team, she'd wanted to do a report on the physics involved in downhill skiing for her science-fair project. When she discovered that someone else had already taken her idea, she decided to report on ski jumping instead. She made a model of a jump hill and everything. The more she got into it, the more jumping fascinated her. She started hanging out at the Olympic Park, watching jump practices, and even convinced her parents to let her try a class or two on the little hills, just to get a feel for what it was like. She'd been hooked ever since.

Part of that had to do with her fascination with the intricate balance of forces required for the perfect jump. Everything had to be just right—equipment, body position, even wind conditions and the configuration of the hill. Coming down the inrun, the jumper had to build up as much speed as possible, relying on gravitational potential energy while still maintaining control. This as she had to shift her body position, starting in a low crouch with her head down like a diver, then adjusting slightly, raising her hips while pressing her chest to her knees, and then rising just a bit more and straightening her arms for the takeoff.

It was that takeoff where all the forces came together. Before she reached the lip of the ramp, the jumper had to push herself up and out in a delicate compromise between needing maximum upward thrust and not letting her body become vertical because that would mess up the forward velocity and cut her distance. And the timing had to be absolutely perfect. Too late and her skis would be pointed upward, resulting in lack of control. Too early and the skis would point down, causing extra wind resistance.

This takeoff was Mo's problem. She could feel it. She just didn't know exactly what it was she was doing wrong.

Riia touched her arm. "Have you seen the *museo* yet? It have very good exhibition on the history of skiing in Finland."

"Hmm? No, I haven't really had the—"

Riia's face lit up. "Come. I show you."

Mo wasn't really in the mood for another museum, but what the heck. She was here already. She might as well.

They walked through the gift shop in front of the museum entrance. "Closing time is near," Riia said, "but we see what we can."

The bright lighting and sleek lines of the *museo* made it look more like an art museum than a history museum. It was divided into two rooms, with a balcony circling above. They paid the fee and Riia hustled Mo into the smaller room. Long rows of display cases lined the walls, featuring memorabilia such as uniforms, event posters, and a collection of skis of various sizes and ages. Those reminded Mo of an evolution illustration showing the metamorphosis of ape to modern man.

"Ski is important part of Finnish history," Riia said. She

pointed to the first display. "That short ski is over four thousand years old."

"Wait. Did you say four *thousand* years old? Not four hundred?"

"Thousand."

"Whoa." Mo stepped closer to examine the ski. It was stubby and fat, probably less than five feet long and over six inches wide. It looked like it had been carved out of wood and, of all the strange things, had some kind of animal fur on the underside. "Um, I'm guessing this thing didn't slide very well over the snow."

Riia nodded. "That ski maybe was more like the snow-shoe. Now look to this pair." She nodded to the next set of skis.

"Those don't look like a pair," Mo said. "One of them is shorter than the other."

"Yes. The long one is called *lyly*. For sliding, you understand? This short one, *kalhu*, push against the snow. Look; the underside has also fur."

"Seems like it would kinda be awkward, pushing and sliding like that."

"Perhaps. Those who used these skis carry one pole to help balance."

Well, that sounded weird. Kinda like the whole concept of one short ski and one long one. "Okay, you got me," she said. "Why did they use just one pole?"

"Come see." Riia pointed to a display of prehistoric-looking ski poles, crudely crafted. At the tip of one, the wood had been filed to a sharp point. On another, a metal spike had been lashed to the wood like a weapon.

Understanding slowly dawned. "The one pole was their spear," Mo said with wonder.

"Yes. Those who used these were hunters. Maybe only in the last hundred years skiers start using two poles. Also, skis became one length."

"So, the hunters didn't use skis anymore?"

"There. You understand." Riia smiled. "This is why ski history has much interest. Changes in skis reflect changes in culture. First it is for walking on snow, then for hunting, then it was become recreation. Skiers find ways to compete. They improve designs of skis until here we have the more modern one."

She pointed to a display case holding what looked like a contemporary Nordic ski, except that it was made out of wood instead of fiberglass.

"This is awesome." Mo turned to Riia. "You've just given me the perfect idea for my paper—Finnish history through ski design. Wouldn't that be cool?"

Riia's eyes lit up. "Yes! It would be...cool. I love skiing history. I help what I can."

"You're on." Mo glanced around. "So what else is there to see in here?"

"The other room have special displays up the stairs and on this floor are many activities."

"Activities?" That's all Mo needed to hear. In the second room, a long white plastic track dominated one half of the room, lined on either side with wooden pine-tree cutouts. A couple of kids were giggling and wobbling along the track on narrow skis, leaning heavily on ski poles.

Just on the other side of the track, a man sat at a table, sighting down the scope of a laser rifle aimed at a target set among yet more cutout trees.

"Biathlon," Riia said. "Also we have the slalom machine and ski jump simulator."

That last one got Mo's attention. "Jump simulator?"

"Yes. Over there."

At the far end of the room, a group of kids and adults were crowded around a wooden booth. Through the large window in the front, Mo could see someone standing inside, and beyond them, some sort of video screen. The person inside the booth hopped up and all the kids started cheering.

"What the...?"

"You have never seen before? We watch."

It was hard to see the screen clearly with so many people crowded around, but it looked like the video on the wall showed the view as a skier raced down a jump hill. When the film reached the end of the ramp, the person in the booth jumped up and then numbers flashed on the screen. It was recording distance!

Mo could hardly contain herself. "What hill is that? How

realistic is it? How does the machine work? Have you done it before?"

Riia laughed. "You are as a little child. Be patient. You will see."

Patience was never Mo's strongest virtue, and waiting for the group to get done was slow torture. There were about fifteen kids and six adults and everyone took a turn, the rest of the group laughing, jeering, and clapping whenever they completed a jump. Mo thought she was going to scream before they had their fill of the simulator and moved on.

At long last, she entered the booth. There wasn't much inside, only a wide, squatty box, some electrical cords, and the monitor. Riia instructed her to stand on the box and face the screen.

The projection began and the screen lit up with the same high-above-it-all scene. Ski tips pointed toward a steep inrun, and below, Mo now recognized the layout of the Sports Center. The film for the simulator must have been shot from the top of the *suurmäki* or the K90.

"Get ready!"

Mo crouched out of habit and watched as the scene on the screen zoomed downward. Her muscles tensed for the takeoff as the film whooshed with the sound of snow under skis and the virtual ski tips approached the takeoff platform. Mo sprang up and the skis on the screen flew out over the knoll. She came down with a thud.

"Oh, no!" Riia giggled as the film showed a wipeout and a lone ski sliding away from the fray. "You jump too soon."

"How does it know?"

"It keep track of when you leave the box. Try again. Watch careful the platform."

Mo crouched on the box again, and tensed as she watched the monitor. She jumped the instant she saw the end of the platform.

Numbers flashed on the screen. Sixty-five meters. "So how'd I do?"

"Good." Riia gave Mo the kind of encouraging smile a teacher might give a five-year-old. "You do good."

"No, really."

Riia shrugged apologetically. "Average jump is eighty to one hundred fifteen meters."

Mo's shoulders slumped. She gestured at the screen. "How can it tell how far I jumped?"

Riia tucked a strand of purple hair behind her ear. "The machine proportion your weight to the force of your legs. It count the time you use for takeoff, and calculate how far such a jump will take you." She shrugged. "You still jump up too soon."

Mo raised her brows and looked back at the screen with renewed interest. That was the exact problem she was having on the real hills. And since she couldn't get more practice time outside, what if she figured out her timing with the machine? It might work.

The lights overhead flickered, startling Mo from her thoughts. "What was that?"

Riia glanced at her watch and frowned. "Closing time. We should go."

Mo followed Riia through the now-deserted *museo*, pausing to take one last look at the ski simulator. Without a doubt, she'd be back.

By Friday, breakfast was becoming an uncomfortable affair. If only the Aaltos wouldn't ask her what her plans were for the day, she wouldn't have to lie. "We have a culture tour to Sibelius Hall and then I was thinking of dropping by the *museo* to work on my report."

Herra Aalto dabbed at the corners of his mouth and laid his napkin back in his lap. "You must be working very hard on it. You've been at the *museo* every night this week."

Mo tried to look him in the eye when she answered, but her guilt wouldn't let her. She stirred the food on her plate instead. Her report on the history of skiing had seemed like the perfect cover for hanging out at the ski museum, but of course she wasn't actually getting any research done, and she was starting to feel bad about lying to Kirsti and her family. Not bad enough to quit, though. The simulator actually seemed to be working. She still landed

short, but she was flying farther. Even Coach Peltonen had noticed. Mo cleared her throat. "I like the museum. There's a lot there to look at."

"Yes, of course," Herra Aalto said proudly, as if the displays at the museum were all his doing. "I admire your dedication."

Mo nodded, but kept her eyes on her plate, unable to accept the compliment openly. What would he say if he knew the great Kip Clark's daughter was trying to improve her jump distance with a simulator? She felt ridiculous even saying it to herself. She couldn't tell them what she was doing. But lying was never justified, was it? She should come clean. Or at least stop sneaking around to the ski museum. As soon as she got the timing of the jump right, that is.

Guilt followed her all morning. In the Finland class, she could hardly concentrate, let alone follow the lesson.

"You should say after me."

"Huh?"

Riia pursed her lips. "The words. I will say and then you say after me."

Mo nodded. "Right. Sorry." She took a deep breath and tried to concentrate.

"What time is it? *Paljonko kello on*?" Riia said.

Mo glanced at her watch. "Almost time to go."

Riia rolled her eyes. "No. Repeat the phrase."

"Oh, yeah. Sorry. *Paljonko kello on*?"

"Good. The time is twenty to eleven. *Kello on kaksikym-mentä vaille yksitoista.*"

"You've got to be kidding me."

"Try to say it."

The bell rang.

"Oh, look at that. It's time to go." Mo jumped up and stuffed her notebook into her backpack. "See you in calc."

"You are ready for the quiz?"

Mo's stomach dropped. "Quiz?"

Riia nodded. "On polynomials and rational functions."

"That's today?"

"It was on the course outline. You did not study?"

"No, I did not. But I can review my notes during computer science."

Cramming an evening's worth of study into one hour didn't do much good; the quiz was a disaster. Professori Hämäläinen instructed the students to correct their own papers and Mo grimaced as each answer was read, realizing just how badly she'd done. They finished up just before the bell rang. The *professori* quickly called out something in Finnish that Mo didn't quite get.

"You need record the score in your notebook," Riia whispered, "then you drop the quiz on the corner of front desk as you leave."

Mo didn't even want to tally up her score, let alone

write it down. Seventy-three percent was just a sneeze away from failing. She quickly folded her paper in half and joined the shuffle of students pushing their way to the *professori's* desk and on out the door. She laid her quiz on the pile of papers and was about to turn away when a hand half hidden by a cuff of black leather reached forward to deposit another paper. Mo glanced down. Leevi Patrin had scored a perfect hundred. Well, what do you know? Underneath that tough exterior, Biker Boy was a math geek! For some reason, Mo found that to be very endearing.

She smiled and glanced up at him. He must have misread her expression because his face hardened and he raised his chin, as if she might challenge him.

"Um, nice job," she said.

His eyes held hers and Mo forgot to breathe. She tried to say more, but her lips felt numb.

The hard lines around his mouth softened into cautiousness and he gave her a tentative smile. "Thanks," he said.

They stood for an awkward moment until someone bumped past Mo to drop off their paper. She stumbled, and when she looked up again, Leevi had started walking away.

"See you at practice," she called. But the moment, whatever it was, was gone.

Chapter Seven

Mo scrutinized each jump as her clubmates went through their rounds. She recognized the aerodynamics in their performance; gravity and air resistance, velocity and friction. She knew when they would come down short or fly the distance. None of it did her any good.

What she could see in watching others jump, she didn't seem to be able to see in herself. No matter how hard she tried, she was still jumping too soon. The simulator confirmed it.

Over the past week, she'd managed to move up a few notches in the girls' ranking, but her ill-timed takeoffs still

put her five notches below Kirsti and six below first place, and that was not going to earn her a forerunner position. She was just going to have to work harder, that's all.

No "cultural activity" was planned for the evening, which meant she could spend more time with the simulator. She kept promising herself each night that she would stop lying to Kirsti and the Aaltos. She hated being dishonest—especially when she and Kirsti were just starting to be friends. But until she nailed the takeoff, she didn't know what else she could do.

The ladies at the *museo* smiled at her when she entered. They were probably wondering about the crazy American and her obsession with their ski machine. Well, give her a few weeks. She'd show them who was crazy when she jumped in the games.

It had been another good session, at least that's what Mo was thinking as she left the simulator. Her distance was consistently getting better, if only by centimeters. She smiled to herself as she bent to pick up her coat and her backpack, but the smile froze on her face when she stood up again. There, across the room but walking purposefully toward her, was Leevi Patrin.

She gave him a weak wave as he approached. "Uh, *hei.*"

"*Hei.*" His eyes went from Mo to the simulator and back

again. He pressed his lips together as if trying to hold back a smile. "What were you doing with that thing?"

"Nothing," she said a little too quickly. "I mean, uh, I was just checking it out. You know, to see how realistic it is."

He raised his brows. "And?"

"And what?"

"How realistic is it?"

She shrugged. "It's okay."

"So, did you improve the timing of your takeoff?"

Mo felt like her face might combust. "My...what?"

"You know"—he leaned close, lowering his voice conspiratorially—"you're never going to get there by playing around with some machine."

"Get where?" she said innocently. "I don't know what you're talking about."

"I could help you better than any machine." He was no longer smiling.

Mo took a step back and looked up...into his velvet-brown eyes. She lost her train of thought. "Um, what?"

"My help," he said simply. "You want it?"

She hesitated. Leevi stepping into the shoes of her dad and her big brothers? Acting all superior and manly with his counsel and advice? Pointing out what she was doing wrong? No, thank you. "What makes you think I need help?"

She regretted the question as soon as it left her lips. It sounded defensive and petulant.

He dropped his hand. "I guess I was wrong. Forget it."

Mo felt an immediate loss at the lack of contact, but she wasn't about to fold. "Forgotten," she said.

Mo sat on the bed that night, books spread out around her, and stared blankly at the far wall. She couldn't concentrate, let alone do her homework. No matter what she did to distract herself, Leevi's mocking smile and dark eyes kept flashing through her head, making her alternately angry and intrigued, and then angry about being intrigued.

She should have known better than to think no one would see her working on the simulator. Everyone in the club hung out at the Sports Center. It was just a matter of time before one of them wandered into the *museo*. Why did it have to be Leevi, though? She was just going to have to figure out some sort of advanced warning system for passing clubmates.

Of course, that wasn't the least of her worries. Sure, she'd improved her distance some over the last couple of weeks, but that would account for only half her total score. There were also style points to think about. The machine had been good for helping her jump at the right time, but it had done nothing for her in-air or landing form. If anything, she was getting clunkier. Kinda the opposite of what she needed to achieve. Her style points were going to be nil.

Finally, she gave up trying to study and pushed her books aside. She needed to do something to chase Leevi's specter out of her head. She glanced at the time. Nine o'clock. That meant it was only noon in Utah. She wanted to talk to Nessa, but Nessa would still be in school. Cell phones weren't allowed at school. Although...twelve o'clock was lunchtime and Nessa usually ate off campus. Maybe Mo would luck out.

She stole a glance at Kirsti—who was working at her computer, headphones on, bopping her head to an unheard beat—and then reached for her cell phone.

nes u there?

mo! wassup? everything ok?

yeah i'm good. u?

good. wots new?

need input

shoot

if u were trying to get ready for a competition and ur jumps reeked and a good looking guy in the club offered 2 give u pointers in private, would u do it?

oh now you have 2 tell me wots going on! do u like him?

sigh yes

he likes u?

Mo thought about that for a moment. How would she know? She was woefully inexperienced. At home she would always hang out with the guys from the ski club because they were "safe." With the clubmate dating ban firmly in place, she never had to worry about who liked whom or any of that kind of stuff. Even outside the team, Mo had no guy skills. How could she have gotten any with her dad and her brothers breathing down her neck all the time?

not sure

how private r these lessons?

secret private

uh oh. mo...be careful

Mo sighed and texted a good-bye. Careful. Right. Story of her life.

Riia caught up with Mo the next morning as they were heading into Finland class. "Where were you last night?"

"Last night?"

"Study group."

Mo's heart dropped. "That was last night?"

Riia didn't have to answer. Her face said it all.

"I'm sorry. I was...caught up in something. I completely forgot."

"*Ei se mitään.*" Riia shrugged. "We can study tonight."

Mo chewed her lip. She should study for her other classes as well—besides the Finnish vocab test coming up, there was the computer science weekly quiz. When was she going to find time for those, let alone math? Especially if she hoped to get in some practice at the *museo*. Something had to give—and it wouldn't be the practice. "I'll let you know," she said.

In computer science, Mo used her class time to study for the upcoming test. She didn't get through the entire outline, but it would have to do. After club practice and the extra time at the *museo*, she'd have a few more hours at home to study. Then there was the quiz and the Linux documentation paper she should have been working on for class... but she could always finish that over the weekend and turn it in late if she had to. And she hadn't even started outlining her history report yet. She frowned. Why didn't these teachers get together and plan their schedules better? How fair was it to have three tests and a paper due in one week?

Riia didn't mention studying again, even in precalc, when Professori Hämäläinen passed out the study guides and reminded the students of their midterm test the following day. In a way, Mo was relieved Riia hadn't brought it up again—saved her the trouble of making up an excuse. On the other hand, she felt bad, like she was letting Riia down.

It wasn't until after practice and a very long session at the *museo* that Mo even cracked the books, and by then, it was hard to focus. She was just on the cusp of getting the takeoff right; she could feel it. All she wanted to do was replay her runs from that afternoon and visualize how she could have improved the jumps. Needless to say, she didn't get much studying done.

Despite the brainless night, Mo didn't think she did too badly on her vocab test. The squaring-functions section of her precalc test, however, completely threw her. She was so embarrassed to hand in her quiz to be marked that she folded it in half so that no one else would see.

Her hands trembled when she took the thing back at the end of class. She glanced over her shoulders before lifting up one corner of the paper to look at the grade. It was worse than she'd imagined; a big red "64" marred the upper right-hand corner. She quickly refolded the paper and stuffed it into her notebook. She'd deal with it later. Right now she had to hustle to the Sports Center and get herself into the zone.

She managed to avoid her clubmates and made it to practice with fifteen minutes to spare. If she hurried and changed and...

"I'm glad to see you here early, Maureen. Could I have a word with you?"

Mo looked up to find Coach Peltonen frowning at her.

Stomach churning ice, she nodded weakly and followed him into the office. He didn't look happy. Whatever was coming couldn't be good.

He held the door open, then motioned for her to have a seat as he took his place behind the desk, shifting in his chair and clearing his throat several times before he spoke.

"Miss Clark," he began. She grimaced, the formality setting her even more on edge. "You do recognize the significance of the word order chosen for the Scholar Athlete Exchange program, yes?"

"The order?"

"The emphasis of the program represented by our moniker. What is the first word?"

Mo looked at her hands. Uh-oh. She knew where this was going. "Um, scholar?"

"That's right. Academics come first. We take our responsibility for the advancement of your education very seriously. Our endorsement by the S.A.S.S. program depends upon it. I've been watching you work with the club and I must say I'm very impressed by your dedication and progress. However..." He shifted again, looking every bit as uncomfortable with delivering the news as Mo was hearing it. "Your teachers report that your marks so far are substandard."

"I know. I'm sorry," Mo said. "I'll do better, I promise."

"I'm sure you will. Your father—"

"Wait. We don't have to tell my dad about this, do we? He'll just get all uptight. I really will try harder."

Coach Peltonen's posture relaxed. Mission accomplished. "Listen, Mo," he said, "grades are important. Not just for this program, but for your academic career. I've seen from your records what you can do. You could have a successful future if you don't allow your priorities to get skewed, understand?"

Mo nodded. She did understand. Coach Peltonen had given her a second chance. There would not be another.

After practice, Mo stayed behind at the gym. She intended to study, she really did, but all she could think about was the time she could be progressing her jumps. Academics might be the number one priority of the SAE program, but *her* number one priority was to jump in the games, and she wasn't going to accomplish that with books. She had to move—to think.

She laced up her Nikes and wandered down the hall to the oldest section of the workout room. It was dark, cold, and deserted, which suited her just fine. She flipped on the lights and turned on a treadmill, stretching her calves as she waited for the digital display to show the machine was ready. Machine. Agh. Did she have to let that word creep into her thoughts? Leevi's voice echoed in her head, *I can help you better than any machine.*

"No thank you." She stepped onto the treadmill and

set the speed for a slow jog to warm up. No way was she going to be the helpless little female to his know-it-all male. Being a girl in this sport was hard enough without adding some guy's machismo to the equation. Besides, this whole thing was about proving to her family that she could make it on her own. She wasn't going to go running for help at the first sign of hardship.

She increased the speed, raised the incline, and ran until her muscles burned and her breath came in ragged, short gasps.

Her mind churned, spinning thoughts as quickly as the rubber tread beneath her feet. She still had six weeks until the games. If she worked hard, she could make a show-ing at the exhibition. But how was she going to be able to concentrate on her schoolwork and figure out her jumps with the limited time she had ahead of her?

Leevi's voice echoed in her head again. *"I can help…"* Her steps slowed and she stumbled, pitching forward as she lost her footing on the treadmill. She managed to slam a palm against the red emergency stop button as she fell to her knees, wheezing and clutching her side.

She knelt on all fours, sweat dripping down her nose, sucking in breath. It always came back to Leevi. Leevi, who Kirsti had called a loser. What if she knew something Mo didn't? On the other hand, what harm would it do to just talk to him? He was one of the best jumpers in the club, and he had offered his services. Accepting his help

wouldn't be the same as falling back on her family, right? It would be her choice. She was being responsible. Yeah. And proactive. The control was still hers.

She pushed shakily to her feet and swiped at her forehead with the back of her hand. Maybe she should see what he had in mind. Couldn't hurt, right?

Chapter Eight

Mo tried to work up the guts to talk to Leevi all day, but this whole going-to-him-for-help thing was turning out to be tougher than she thought. What was she supposed to say that didn't make her sound like she was a complete loser?

In calc she made eye contact with him, but that was as far as it went. He looked at her with those espresso-colored eyes and she almost forgot what she needed to talk to him about.

Until practice, that is, where Coach Peltonen kept

watching as if he could discern what kind of an effort she was making in school just by looking at her, and where she jumped worse than ever. Sure, maybe it was just nerves, but it was enough to make Mo swallow her pride and go hunting for Leevi the moment practice was over.

She found him walking across the parking lot in front of the stadium. "Hey, Leevi," she called, "wait up!"

He turned and looked at her with an unreadable expression on his face. Swallowing the urge to forget the whole thing, she ran to catch up with him. Unfortunately, the parking lot was more like a skating rink—covered in ice. She hit a slick spot and sprawled at Leevi's feet.

"Are you all right?" He dropped his bag and bent to help her, acting like he was all concerned and everything, though he didn't bother to hide the laughter in his eyes.

She just about refused his hand, but then she had to concede that it probably did look funny, and she really did need his help, so she allowed him to pull her to her feet. Nothing injured. Just her backside and her pride.

"You think that was good," she said, "you should see my follow-up act."

His lips curved into a...she swallowed...very nice smile. And she realized that he was still holding her hand. She froze, uncertain of what to do next.

Leevi cocked his head to the side. "So," he said, drawing out the single syllable so that it became question and statement all at once.

Mo cleared her throat. She wanted to pull her hand away from his, but then again she didn't. "Um." She hesitated one final moment and then rushed ahead before she lost her nerve. "I was thinking, you know, about what you said last week and, um, I was wondering if you would still be willing, I mean, if the offer is still open, I was just thinking that I really could use some help, you know, and so I thought maybe, if you had time and all, maybe you...I...I mean, do you think you still have time?" Oh, yeah. Brilliant orator.

"You want me to help you with the jumping."

"Um, yeah," she squeaked. "That was kinda the idea."

He nodded. "Yeah. All right."

"Really?" She smiled with relief. "That is so great. Thanks."

"It's okay. It'll be good for my résumé."

At first she thought he was joking. She laughed and he let go of her hand. His usual guarded look had returned.

"You really have a résumé?"

He shrugged. "University applications."

"Oh. Is that why you help Coach Peltonen?"

"Pretty much."

"So you don't mind. Helping me, I mean."

"Are you kidding? It's gotta look good to say I worked with Kip Clark's daughter."

Mo felt as if he'd just dumped ice over her. She should have known. It always came back to that.

"There's something else..." He cleared his throat. "Something you can do for me."

She stiffened. "What?"

He studied his feet. "I could...use some visibility. You know, to help with the college apps. Do you think, maybe, you could get some publicity for me at the games?"

Mo laughed. "You're delusional. What makes you think I could get anyone publicity?"

"Oh, come on," he said. "With a family like yours—"

She didn't need to hear any more. She turned on her heel and walked—carefully this time—away.

"Hey, Clark," Leevi called.

"Forget it!"

He caught up with her before she reached the side-walk. "What's the problem? You have the name, I have the know-how. We help each other out. Win-win all around."

She turned to face him. "No, Leevi. You don't get it. You win. I lose."

"No, I *don't* get it." His voice hardened. "It's a simple proposition. I help you get what you want, and you help me get what I want. Neither one of us has to enjoy the process, but we'll both be happier in the end."

He held out his hand and she looked at it for a long moment. He was right. Reporters *were* always hanging around after competitions, sniffing for the next Clark news item. Getting the publicity wasn't the hard part. Avoiding it was.

She had to decide—which did she value more, having a shot at jumping in the games, or maintaining her autonomy apart from the family legacy? Did she really have a choice? If she didn't do *something*, she was going to fail. What good would her independence do her then?

With a resigned sigh, she shook his hand. She had just sealed the bargain—and that's not even the thing that bothered her most.

Did he just say he wouldn't enjoy helping her?

The next evening at practice, Mo sat on the start bar, knots tightening in her stomach as she waited for the signal. She had an extra reason to be nervous about this jump: Leevi was standing at the bottom, watching her. Well, technically, the guys had always been watching when the girls jumped and vice versa, but this time, Mo *knew* he was watching her—and that he would be scrutinizing her every move. Yes, she knew he had to figure out what she was doing wrong before he could help her, but she didn't know she'd be so self-conscious when the moment came.

At the signal, Mo slid away from the bar. She kept her sights on the takeoff ramp and let her training take over. Crouch, zoom, jump, fly. It felt like a good jump. One look at Coach Peltonen's face, however, and she knew she wasn't quite getting it. She didn't even want to know her distance. Or to look in Leevi's direction.

At the top of the outrun, she slid sideways to a stop and

quickly undid her bindings so she could step off her skis. All she wanted to do was slink away and hide in a corner. Coach Peltonen had other ideas.

"One more time," he called, waving her toward the hill. "You're just about there!"

Mo let her eyes slide over to where Leevi was leaning against the fence, face set in an exasperatingly unreadable expression. He met her gaze and gave her an almost imperceptible nod. She blinked. What? Did he think she was looking to him for permission? Grinding her teeth, she swung her skis up onto her shoulders. She tried to stalk to the side of the outrun, but between the snow and her ski boots, she was pretty sure it looked more like a demented march. He might be helping her with a few style pointers, but she did not need his go-ahead for anything.

Her last jump was even worse, which, of course, was all Leevi's fault. He was psyching her out. How could she fly when she was all tense? Maybe this whole thing wasn't such a good idea. After practice she'd have to talk to him and tell him the deal was off.

Mo waited until everyone else had cleared the stadium before she went looking for Leevi. She may have decided to enlist his help, but she didn't want the whole club to know about it. She found him outside, settling a wooden box into the snow. He looked up and gave her a nod in acknowledgment.

"One of your problems," he said, "is vision. You're anticipating the takeoff instead of seeing it." He stood and held his hand out to her. "Come here."

Wait. She was going to tell him the deal was off, right? But he was already set. Maybe after this one session. She stepped up onto the box. Okay, she could do this. It was nothing new; they did the same kind of technique exercise in Park City. She crouched into her inrun position without having to be told.

Leevi grunted his approval. He walked around her, straightening her arms, adjusting the angle of her head. "You want to look up, but keep your head down. Visualize where you want to go."

Mo nodded and stared straight ahead. Leevi stepped into view. He positioned himself in front of her with out-stretched arms.

"Okay. When you're ready," he said.

She hesitated. It was one thing to jump into the arms of your coach, quite another to jump into the arms of—she might as well face it—an abundantly hot if annoyingly unreadable clubmate. But the look on his face was all business. For all intents and purposes, he *was* her coach. Kind of.

She took a deep breath of the frozen air and released it slowly, visualizing the muscles in her legs like coils, tightening, strength gathering for the moment of release. And then, keeping her sights focused ahead, she sprang

up from the crouch and launched herself forward, body rigid, arms straight to her side, feet flexed and angled outward. Leevi caught her at the hips and held her above his head for several seconds before setting her gently to the ground.

"Good, but you need more power into it. Try it again."

Mo nodded. Okay. He wanted power? He'd get power. She crouched again, summoning every last ounce of strength in her body to jump up and out from the block. He caught her again, only let her down more slowly this time. Or was that just her imagination? Was it because her heart was doing a sprint around her chest, constricting her lungs so that she could hardly breathe? Was it because she *wanted* him to have set her down slowly?

When he set her on her feet, she took a shaky step backward. "How was that?" she managed to ask.

He blew out a breath. "Better, but we're going to have to spend some time strength training to get more power in your legs. And you've really got to get that forward motion when you're coming up. Let's try it one more time."

Mo slipped into the apartment as quietly as she could, but Herra Aalto heard her right away. "Maureen," he called. "Is that you? Come on into the dining room."

She swallowed. "Coming." It felt like a lump of ice had settled in her stomach. She was so busted. Her session with Leevi had taken longer than her visits at the *museo* normally did. She should have called. She hung up her coat slowly and straightened her boots under the bench. This was not going to be good.

"Yes?" she said as she came into the room.

"Ah, there you are. Your father called. Brilliant man. Brilliant." Herra Aalto's eyes lit up like a little kid. Kirsti had called it right; her dad was a Kip Clark groupie. "Said he hadn't heard from you in a while, though. Wanted me to remind you to write. You are hereby reminded."

"Oh. Yeah. Thanks." Huh. He hadn't even noticed the time. If it had been Kirsti standing there, he'd have been all over her, reminding her she needed her rest while she was in training. Just like Mo's dad would have done if she had been back home. She said good night and slumped back to her room.

Kirsti glanced up as she entered. "Where were you? I looked for you in the locker room."

Mo hesitated. She didn't want to start lying to Kirsti again. First the *museo* and now Leevi. The former was bad enough, although even if she thought it was dumb, Kirsti would probably understand. But the latter...Kirsti had warned Mo about Leevi. She obviously didn't like the guy. What would she say if she knew Mo would be spending all her free time with him? Especially if she knew Mo was doing it to become greater competition?

"Oh, I had to talk to the coach." Well, it wasn't exactly a lie. She *had* talked to the coach. Just not that day.

Kirsti nodded sympathetically. Even though she had never said anything, she had to have noticed how abysmal Mo's performance on the hill had been.

"Was it helpful?"

Mo thought of Leevi—working with her only because of what he could get out of it. Not the strongest recommendation by a long shot. But then she remembered the feel of his hands on her waist, the feather of his breath on her cheek. "I'm not sure," she said.

"Oh. Well, you still have time until the competition. You just need to get some sleep and forget about it."

"Thanks, I will."

But Mo couldn't sleep. She kept thinking about her deal with Leevi. She needed to call it off. Clubmate and crush interest was never a good combination. Especially when she was the only one crushing.

Mo avoided Leevi the next day, sitting clear on the other side of the room in calculus while purposely avoiding the merest glance in his direction, and hanging back in practice so that they wouldn't find themselves close enough to actually converse. Of course, after practice and the requisite cultural outing, she had no choice. They were scheduled to meet, and he'd been waiting for her. What was she supposed to do, stand him up?

When she saw him, her resolve to cancel their arrangement began to crumble. He looked so serious. It would be really mean to pull out on him, right? Maybe if she was just careful to keep her distance...

"We're going to work on strength today," he said as she neared.

How appropriate.

"When you are jumping, you want all the power to come from here." He wrapped both of his hands around his thigh. Mo nodded breathlessly. "If you use your lower legs for thrust, you run the risk of pushing off the balls of your feet, and then your skis will point down. You don't want that."

Yeah, Mo knew all that.

"We'll start with cardio and then work on weights."

"But isn't the building closed?"

He dangled a set of keys. "My cousin's a custodian."

"Oh." She followed him to the deserted gym, running the words she needed to say through her head. *This isn't such a good idea... this isn't such a good idea... this isn't such a good idea.*

He led her to the treadmill and she mentally rolled her eyes. Oh, yes. Like she couldn't have done this on her own. She stepped up anyway, and started the belt rotating.

Leevi climbed on the treadmill beside her and set the machine to a gentle run, instructing her to do the same.

"You should be able to carry on a conversation."

"Okay."

"So start talking."

"What?"

He gave her one of his soul-piercing looks without even breaking his stride. "I want to see that you can do it. Talk to me."

"What do you want me to say?"

"Tell me why you want to jump in the Lahti Games so bad."

"Are you kidding?"

"No."

She clenched her jaw and concentrated on her stride. This was going to be harder than she'd thought. Did she really want to broadcast her insecurities in front of this guy?

"Anytime you're ready."

"Okay. Here it is. Women's ski jumping has been held back long enough. It's time to start knocking the barriers to the ground, and I want to be the one with the sledge-hammer."

"That's very poetic. What's the real story?"

She gave him a sidelong glance and sighed. "All right. I want to do something that no one else in my family has done. That's pretty hard in a family of overachievers. You know about my dad, but the rest of my family—"

"Two brothers are Olympic medalists, a couple are

snowboard champions, the rest top skiers in their class. Did I leave anything out?"

Mo scowled and stared straight ahead. For someone who had done his homework, he was pretty stupid. "No, you got it all, except for how it feels to have people base their expectations about who you are and what you can do on who your family is."

"Actually, I get that, too." He stared straight ahead. "You're starting to sound winded. Take it down a notch and keep talking."

She obediently adjusted the speed.

"How about you? Why don't you tell me what you plan to do with this media coverage you want me to arrange?"

He shrugged. "A little visibility might help me get a scholarship to an American university."

"America? Why do you want to go there? Why not go to university here?"

"I told you. To train."

"But why—"

He clenched his jaw. "Because my last name is Patrin, okay? It's not easy for our kind here."

"Your kind?"

"*Roma. Mustalaiset.* Gypsies."

She blinked, thinking uneasily about what Kirsti had said. "I...I didn't think that mattered here. I mean, Finland is a very progressive society."

"You're starting to sound winded again."

"No, I'm not."

"Yes, you are. Stop talking."

"Ha. Nice try. You're trying to change the subject."

"Let's drop it."

"Hey, you think you have the corner on discrimination? I wanted to get away from Utah because my last name is Clark. People judge me by my family name, too. And I know all about discrimination. I don't get to compete in the games because I'm a girl, remember?"

"That's not discrimination, that's tradition."

"Oh, give me a break. So is looking down on certain ethnic groups. That doesn't make it right."

He regarded her for several strides. "You have a point," he said simply. "Enough running for now. Let's go work on weights."

Mo sat at the lat machine, hands clenched around the foam rubber grips on the bar. Leevi hadn't spoken much since the treadmill, except to remind her about proper lifting form and to ask if he could add more weight. As annoying as he had been before, she preferred his words to his silence.

"So…" Her voice strained as she struggled to pull the bar down behind her head. "You don't need me to carry on a conversation with the weights, huh?"

He pressed his lips together, but couldn't hide his smile. "Well, if you want to talk to the weights, go ahead."

"You're very funny."

"Whatever you say."

It wasn't quite as easy to talk while she was doing reps, but Mo didn't want Leevi to lapse into silence again. She kept up an ongoing dialogue on everything from the difficulty of the Finnish language to her impatience with Herra Kolehmainen's cultural outings.

"We can't even see half the places he takes us to because it's already dark by the time we finish practice. Like that park with all the sculptures covered in snow. What was the point of that?"

Leevi looked up. "The Lanu sculptures?"

"Yeah, I think that's what they were called."

He nodded. "I did a paper on Olavi Lanu for an art history class. He was a real deep artist. Very symbolic. But you really need to see the sculptures in the light. What about Saturday before practice?"

"What about it?"

"We'll go see the park the way it's meant to be seen."

"Oh. I...um..."

"Are you doing anything Saturday morning?"

"No..."

"Okay. It's a date. And then we can work on the small jumps before practice."

Mo flushed. Okay, so she knew he was just milking his role as the great benevolent wise one who was going to put an end to her cultural deficiencies, but for the moment she was just going to enjoy the thought; she had a date with Leevi Patrin.

Chapter Nine

Saturday morning, Mo slipped out of the room while Kirsti was doing her homework. She told Rouva Aalto she was going to the Sports Center early to get in a little extra work before regular practice. Leevi *had* mentioned putting in time on the small hills, so as long as she did that, it wasn't technically a lie.

The sun was just coming up when Leevi met her at the main bus station. The park wasn't far from there, just off the harbor. As they walked to the entrance, the insulation of newly fallen snow hushed the sounds of the city and draped the park in silence.

"Are you sure we should be here?" Mo whispered. "It looks closed. There's no one else around."

"This is the perfect time to see the sculptures, when the snow is fresh and undisturbed." Leevi pushed her forward when she held back.

"You didn't answer my question."

"It's fine." He prodded her along the winding path. "Don't worry. If anyone gives us a problem, I'll just tell them I'm your tutor."

"Oh, right. Like anyone's going to..." Her voice trailed off as the first enormous sculpture loomed before them, snow-shrouded and graceful.

"You like it?"

"I can't tell. It's...um...covered in snow."

"Exactly." Leevi studied the snowy hulk, moved a few steps to his left, then studied it some more. Finally he spoke. "This is how they're supposed to be. The sculptor, Lanu, wanted his sculptures to be natural, to blend with the surroundings. They're best when they're draped in snow in the winter or vines in the summer."

Mo tilted her head, looking at the twisted snow mass from a different angle. "Okay. Why?"

Leevi's face lost its usual guarded look. He thought for a moment. "Lanu's works are like an invitation for man to get closer to nature instead of fighting against it."

Mo stared at him. She gestured at the hidden statue. "You get that from this?"

He shrugged. "Yeah."

She shook her head.

"What?"

"Just...you surprise me."

He seemed to think about that for a moment, then grinned. "Come on. I want to show you the rest."

They wandered through the park, Leevi nudging Mo from time to time to examine a sculpture. Despite long stretches of silence, Mo felt completely comfortable. Even when she slipped on a downward slope of the path and Leevi caught her to save her from falling. He kept one hand protectively at the small of her back as they ambled on. The gesture didn't make her feel giddy or rapturous, just...safe.

"Tell me more about your family," he said after one long stretch of silence. "What's it like to constantly be in their shadow?"

She slowed her step. "You know, you're the first one who has ever asked me that. Everyone assumes we're all one unit, like we all act the same and feel the same..." She looked up at him. "It's hard sometimes."

He nodded.

"But you already know all about my family. What about yours? What are they like? Where do you live?"

Leevi stopped in the middle of the path and looked at her. "You really want to know?"

"I wouldn't have asked if I didn't."

He shrugged. "We're pretty average, I guess. I have two older brothers."

"And?"

"My grandmother lives with us."

"What else?"

"Not much more to tell. My mother works at Lahti Glass Works and Father is an engineer." He looked out across the snow, the little muscle at the corner of his jaw twitching. There was something he wasn't saying.

"Sounds...nice."

He ran a hand over the back of his neck. "Yeah. Most of the time. Except that when I was growing up, my dad couldn't always keep a job. He was...sick a lot of the time."

"What was wrong?"

A shadow passed over his face. He looked into Mo's eyes for a long time before speaking. "Alcohol."

"Oh, I'm sorry."

"It's okay." He kicked at the snow. "I understand it now, but when I was growing up I hated him for it. It made us look like the Gypsy stereotype, moving from place to place, my mother and grandmother selling handwork when money got tight..."

He bent and gathered a fistful of snow, but it was too cold and wouldn't pack. He let it sift through his fingers, then brushed off his hands and turned back to Mo. "Our people don't all travel around in caravans, you know. We don't all beg or steal, but that's what people expect. The government says they have to treat us equally. They make laws for our 'benefit' as a minority, but those kinds of things just make people resent us. Like, the public schools were required to teach us in our native tongue, Kàlo Finnish. It cost a lot of money, so people hated us for that. But I hated the special treatment. I just wanted to be like everyone else."

"That I can understand," Mo said softly.

Leevi gave her half a smile and nodded. "Now come on. Let's see the rest." He grew quiet as they walked the remainder of the path.

As they were about to leave, one of the sculptures caught Mo's attention. She wasn't sure what it was supposed to be under the snow, but in its present state, it looked like a twisted white arch and she liked the movement of it.

She pulled out her notebook and pencil to write a comment about it. Finally! She was inspired to make a spontaneous entry into her *Suomen päiväkirja*.

She had to pull off one glove so that she could grip her pencil and the cold immediately pinched her skin. She tried to write quickly before her fingers froze. Leevi leaned close to read what she was writing. Her heart skipped as she felt him behind her. And again when he reached over her shoulder to point at her paper. "You spell his first name with only one *i*."

Even through her scarf, Mo could feel the warmth of Leevi's breath on her cheek. It made her stomach do a little flip that was not altogether unpleasant. "One *i*," she murmured.

He nodded in agreement and drew back his hand, the fingertips of his gloves brushing over her thumb.

More flipping.

She hoped he didn't notice the way her hand shook as she changed the spelling. She turned her head to see if he was looking and found his face close. So close. Her breath mingled with his. He met her eyes, surprised at first, and then...there was something else. He blinked and pulled back quickly.

"Right." His voice became rough. "We should hurry back to the Sports Center so you can get a couple of runs on the hills before practice."

Mo stuffed her notebook back into her pocket as they walked back to the exit gates. She touched his arm. "Thanks for coming with me, Leevi. This was exactly what I needed."

"Hei," he said. "That's what tutors are for."

Mo's face fell. "Right."

When they got to practice, Leevi made no sign of having just spent the morning with Mo. He didn't really ignore her, but he wasn't exactly going out of his way to talk to her, either. He was too busy helping Coach Peltonen critique everyone's form as they worked on the boxes and the ramps, warming up for the jumps. When it came her turn to step up onto the box, it was like he didn't even know her, the way he acted—impersonal, polite, detached.

Mo tried to adopt his same nonchalance without being obvious, but she must not have been doing a very good job because Riia noticed something was up right away.

"Don't let him bother you. He is the same with everyone."

"I'm sorry?"

Riia lowered her voice. "Leevi's family has no money. He must help Coach Peltonen to pay for training and he does not like it more than anyone else."

Raising her brows, Mo looked back to Leevi again. He'd said he was doing it to build his résumé. But given what she'd learned about his family, the money thing made sense. Was that why some of the local club members seemed to look down on him, even though he was the best jumper of the group? The more she got to know him, the more she realized there was a lot to learn about Leevi Patrin.

The next Friday before school, Mo stole a moment on the computer while Kirsti was in the shower. Time had been passing faster than Mo could keep up with it. Another

week gone and she was falling further and further behind. She hardly had time to think, but she knew if she didn't write the stupid weekly e-mail to her parents, they'd probably wig out and call the Aaltos again. Besides, they'd been writing to her nearly every day and she was beginning to feel guilty. She sighed and began to type.

To: kclark@email.com
From: mntmojo@email.com
Subject: Weekly Report

Dear Mom and Dad,

Moikka! That's "hi" in Finnish. How are things going? Still really busy here. This Thursday is Kalevala day. The Kalevala is like Finnish mythology. Sounds interesting, but can you believe they made a national holiday around it? Instead of school, we'll go to Helsinki for the day to look at Kalevala art in some museum.

Yesterday we went to a place called—are you ready for this?—Pro Puu. LOL (*Puu* means "wood" in Finnish.) It was actually pretty cool, though. It's in an old match factory building down by the harbor and they had all sorts of wood things on display from boats to toys to furniture.

The big Kemi trip is coming up in a few weeks, so we are starting to study more about northern Finland. That's pretty cool, too. Or cold. Hehe

That's about it for this week.

Gotta run to school.

Hugs and all that mushy stuff,

Mo

In Overview of Finland, Herra Kolehmainen pumped up the class for the upcoming Kalevala day, or *Kalevalan päivä*, as he called it.

"The Kalevala is more than just mythology; it encompasses the very essence of the Finnish people," he said, "from the creation of the world and the origin of man, to the quest for knowledge and power." He explained how the Kalevala stories were shared through song for generations until a man named Elias Lönnrot collected and compiled them in written form. *Kalevalan Päivä* was a commemoration of the first publication of this collection.

"This class will celebrate the day with a field trip to the *kansallismuseo*," he continued. "That's the National Museum in Helsinki, for those of you who have not read your syllabus."

He picked up a sheaf of papers and began distributing them on desks as he talked, describing the special Kalevala exhibition at the *museo*. "By the time we are through, you should be able to complete the worksheet attached to your itinerary."

Mo quickly shuffled her papers to find one listing the main players in the Kalevala saga. She groaned. There were so manyl

"All of these characters can be found represented in the artwork throughout the museum," Herra Kohlemainen continued. "Your grade in this unit will be greatly enhanced if you can list who they are and where you found them. To complete this cultural outing, you will write an insightful essay on the significance of the Kalevala to Finns today. Any questions?"

Riia's hand shot up. "This free time listed on the itinerary...will we be able to explore the city?"

Herra Kohlemainen nodded. "Once you have completed the worksheet, the remaining time is yours to do with as you please, so long as you meet back up with the group at the appointed time for the trip back to Lahti."

Riia grinned and nudged Mo. "Shopping," she mouthed.

"Now..." Herra Kohlemainen perched on the edge of his desk. "Before our adventure on Thursday, let's talk about some of the stories and characters from the Kalevala so that you will be able to appreciate what you see." He held up a picture of an old man dressed in long robes, white hair hanging in tendrils around his shoulders. "This is the Kalevala hero Väinämöinen. Does he look familiar to any of you?"

One of the guys raised his hand. "Yeah. He looks like that guy in *Lord of the Rings.*"

"That is exactly right. Did you know that J.R.R. Tolkein

studied the Kalevala before writing his *Lord of the Rings* books? It is widely held that Väinämöinen's character directly influenced his creation of Gandalf. Here's another interesting fact; he also studied Finnish before his creation of the *Lord of the Rings*' High Elvish language, Quenya."

Well, Mo had to admit the Tolkein connection was pretty cool, but she still wasn't thrilled to add more study to her already backlogged list of homework.

Riia seemed excited about the prospect of a trip to Helsinki, though. She couldn't stop talking about it all day. "Shopping Helsinki is the best. There has many more stores than Lahti."

Her enthusiasm eventually caught hold of Mo as well. "Well, I do need to look for something for my family, and for my best friend back home."

"Then it is perfect day!"

Mo started her "perfect day" that Thursday by being late. Rouva Aalto had to drive her to the train station because she didn't have time to take the bus.

"I hope you enjoy the *Kansallismuseo*. It is included in our Walking Tour of Helsinki information, you know." She tapped a glossy trifold pamphlet on the seat between them. "If you look just across the street, you will see a white building of granite and marble. That is the *Finlandia Talo*, the famous concert hall designed by Alvar Aalto.

Would you like to take one of the pamphlets? It may be of some use if you decide to walk around a bit afterward." She checked her rearview mirror and changed lanes, frowning. "I would have preferred for Kirsti to show you around."

Mo picked up the pamphlet. "It's okay. Since she's not in the class, this trip was optional for her. It's probably nice for her to sleep in."

Rouva Aalto nodded, but Mo knew she wasn't happy that Kirsti had refused to get out of bed that morning. The ensuing argument was the reason Mo had been late. In truth, she really didn't mind that Kirsti stayed behind. She didn't seem all that comfortable with Riia, so it might have been a little awkward going shopping afterward.

Riia met Mo at the front doors of the station and helped her navigate the ticket machines. The train was already on the platform when they caught up with the rest of the class. They settled into their seats just as it pulled out of the station.

Outside the window, snow-shrouded scenery rolled by—slowly at first and then faster as the train picked up speed until hills, trees, and shadows undulated past the window like a great white-and-gray sea. Ice had crusted on the power lines above the train and sparks flashed, lighting the predawn landscape as the connector passed along the wires so that the scene flickered like an old-time movie. It was hypnotic. Sedative. The hour passed in a blur, and soon trees gave way to houses and houses gave way to buildings and the train rolled into the Helsinki station.

Riia jumped to her feet the moment it stopped. "Quick! The *museo*, and then we shop!"

Four hours later, Mo and Riia settled into a couple of molded plastic chairs in the eatery of the Forum Mall. Riia boasted that Forum housed over one hundred stores, and Mo smiled halfheartedly. Any other time, the prospect of so many places to shop might have been exciting, but after their whirlwind tour of the *museo*, Mo just felt overwhelmed. They had raced from room to room, identifying and scribbling down Kalevala characters' names until they all ran together in Mo's mind.

At least she could relax a little in the familiarity of her current surroundings. The food court looked exactly like the ones found in American malls. There was even one vendor selling southern fried chicken, and the Hesburger looked very much like a McDonald's. Mo tried their *ruis-filehampurilainen*, a rye-bread hamburger, which was actually very good.

Picking at her fries, she looked over the Kalevala worksheet and noticed a blank space on her page. "Oh, no. I'm missing Aino."

Riia glanced at her own paper. "She was in the Keinäinen painting in the second room."

"Thanks." Mo scribbled in the information. "Now I just have to figure out something to write for the essay."

Riia shook her head. "No! No writing. All the weekend is for you to do that. We are here to shop."

"Relax. I just want to get the idea percolating in my head so that when I *do* write it, I'll know what to say."

"Well, that is simple. Just say the story of the Kalevala tell of hardships and many trials and shows the *sisu* of the Finnish people."

Mo looked up from her paper. "*Sisu?* What's that?"

"It can mean many thing—stubborn, strong, determined, persevering." Riia shrugged. "It is who we are. We Finns are very proud of our *sisu.*"

Mo turned the word over in her head. It sure seemed to cover a lot of what she'd seen since she'd come to Finland: Kirsti and her stubbornness with her parents, Riia sticking with practice even when she'd been hurt, Leevi and his determination not to be held back by his family name. That last thought made Mo's face grow warm. She took a quick sip of her soda. "So…" She cleared her throat. "What about this? In my essay I could say that to know the Kalevala is to know *sisu* and to know *sisu* is to know Finland."

"Yes. Good. Now no more school talk! We are here to shop."

Mo raised her hands in mock surrender and then made

a big show of tucking her paper away. "Okay." She picked up her hamburger. "We know what I need to get. What are you looking for?"

"Where?"

"Here. At the mall. What do you want to buy?"

Riia's smile turned secretive. In her felt hat with the earflaps and braided trim and her bright green eyes gazing off beyond Mo's head, she looked like some kind of Nordic Mona Lisa. "Nothing special."

"Oh, no you don't." Mo put her burger down. "You're up to something. What is it?"

Riia looked over her shoulder then leaned across the table, eyes alight. "You never tell. Promise?"

"My lips are sealed."

"Tapio has the name day soon. I will look for a gift."

Mo shook her head. "What's name day?"

"In Finland, we celebrate the name like the birth. You do not do this in America?"

"No. But it sounds cool. So, Tapio, huh? So, um…you like him?"

Riia shrugged and looked away, but she couldn't hide the smile on her face.

"You do! You *like* him." Mo could totally picture the two of them together. "Does he know?"

Riia's eyes widened. "No! You will not tell?"

"I promise." She toyed with the straw in her drink. "So,

is it hard, you know, with him being a clubmate and all? I mean, you see him all the time..."

"Yes. No. I like to be near."

"And, um, is it generally okay over here for clubmates to date?"

Riia shrugged. "I never have gone the date before, so I do not know." She blew out a breath. "The coach will say for not to date. He does not like complications."

That's what Mo was afraid of.

"And now..." Riia wadded her burger wrap into a ball. "We shop!"

They took the escalator to the top floor, where Riia dragged Mo from store to store, sniffing out sales like a bloodhound. She slowed only three times, once to grab a clearance sweater at H&M, once to buy purple nail polish at a cosmetics store whose name Mo couldn't pronounce, and once again at the littala glass boutique.

That last one was for Mo.

She was mesmerized by the rows and rows of everything glass—from vases to plates to candleholders. Mo especially liked the colored-glass votive holders she found in one corner of the store.

"This design is 'Kivi,'" Riia said. "It is very popular for gift."

Mo loved the way the texture of the glass multiplied the

light of the small candle within and cast glowing shadows around itself. She sorted through the colors until she came up with one called Roseolive.

"Look at this." She held it up. "Isn't that cool?" As she moved it in and out of the light, the glass took on different hues, from yellow, to green, to rose.

Mo bought two, one for herself and one for Nessa.

"Kamppi next," proclaimed Riia, "and then Sokos and Stockmann's. Hurry! We have not much time!"

Riia fretted all afternoon about finding the perfect gift for Tapio and finally settled on a knit hat with a wild design. "We are done!" she said. "Unless you have more shop?"

"No, I'm good. How are we doing for time?"

Riia consulted her watch and hissed in a breath. "It is almost four! We have only ten minutes until the train leave!"

They ran through the frozen afternoon twilight, slipping and giggling, all the way to the train station, but as they neared one set of doors, Riia slowed.

"We should use other entrance." She glanced nervously at two ladies in colorful, full skirts who huddled near the doorway, clutching heavy woolen shawls around their shoulders as they offered works of embroidery to travelers who rushed in or out of the station.

Mo tried not to stare. "Wait. Are those Gypsies?"

"Yes. I don't like to pass them by, especially when the children come with their little hands out. You must ignore. You cannot give them money or they never leave you."

"That's sad."

"That they beg?"

"That you have to ignore them."

"Well, you don't want to be rude, but they may steal from you, yes? Some ladies go into stores and hide goods in their skirts. It is big problem." Riia ushered her to another entrance. "We should hurry or we are late."

Mo took one last look at the Gypsy ladies, and wondered if she should buy something from them, but Riia grabbed her arm and dragged her onto the train. She dropped into her seat and watched out the window, catching her breath as she waited for the train to leave the station.

Then, at the far end of the platform, a swish of color caught her eye. She pressed her forehead against the cold glass to watch as an old Gypsy woman climbed aboard the last car. A tall boy with brown hair, dark jeans, and a black leather jacket gently held her arm. He glanced up and Mo's breath caught. Leevi!

She pulled back from the window, a weird, sinking feeling in her chest. Seeing him with the old lady stirred up all sorts of confusion in her head.

She remembered what he had said about his mother and grandmother having to sell handwork. Like the Gypsies outside the station. For the first time, she understood the kind of prejudice he had been talking about. If she was to be completely honest with herself, she had to admit she had felt a kind of superior pity for those women. What's more, she had allowed herself to feel gracious for having the charity to pity them. Now a gnawing sense of shame created a hollow feeling in her stomach.

Maybe she had more lessons to learn than just about the Kalevala and *sisu*.

Chapter Ten

Mo felt awkward around Leevi after that trip to Helsinki. She worked extra hard in their practices together, trying to mask her confusion.

If Leevi noticed anything different in the way she was acting, he never mentioned it. In fact, he had only positive things to say as the week passed and it was obvious that she was getting more confident about her jumps. Eventually she relaxed, but she could never fully forget.

On Friday evening, he was especially attentive, carrying her bag and walking her to the bus stop after their session. "What time tomorrow? Club practice is early because of the coach's meeting. I have to go to that, but then after-ward—"

"I can't. I'm going to the lake house with the Aaltos tomorrow night."

He frowned. "I forgot. When will you be back?"

"I'm not sure. Sunday sometime. What's your number? I could call you."

"No," he said quickly. "I'm...not sure I'll be home."

"Oh." She dug her hands into her pockets and kicked her toe against a ridge of ice on the sidewalk. "So... coach's meeting, huh?"

"Yeah. Exhibition's just over three weeks away."

"I see." She heard the distant diesel rumble of the bus. "So I guess I'll see you Monday, then?"

He nodded.

A bus turned the corner and began lumbering down the street toward them. "My bus," she said.

He handed the bag to her. Was it her imagination, or did his hand linger on hers for an extra moment when she took it? She couldn't help but smile. "Thanks."

The smile faded when she climbed onto the bus. There, sitting in the third row back, was Kirsti.

"*Hei.*" Mo tried to sound natural and breezy as she dropped onto the seat beside her. "What are you doing here? I thought you went home a while ago."

"I had things to do in town." Kirsti cocked her head. "Was that Leevi Patrin I just saw you with?"

"Uh, yeah. I...ran into him after—"

"Watch out for him."

Kirsti's face was completely serious. Mo shook her head. "Oh, hey. He was just—"

"I wasn't kidding before when I said you should stay away from him. Just be careful."

"Careful," Mo agreed. "Eyes wide open."

Herra and Rouva Aalto picked up Mo and Kirsti directly from practice Saturday afternoon to drive to the lake. Mo watched out the window as the city lights disappeared behind them and then read road signs aloud as they passed each one, practicing her pronunciation. Her favorite had to be the yellow triangle moose-crossing signs. She didn't know why, but for some reason those struck her as funny.

After about an hour or so, Herra Aalto pulled off the main road and guided his 4x4 down a narrow snow-packed lane. His high beams reflected so brightly off the white that Mo had to squint to see. After what seemed like a long time, she caught sight of a large wooden house tucked in among the trees. As they pulled closer, she could see that drifts of snow had swept onto a covered porch that was supported by carved, wooden poles and that the trim beneath the eaves was crusted with ice. She could make out a smaller structure just beyond the main house—also log, but without the fancy carving.

"Welcome to our *möki*," Herra Aalto said as he killed the engine. "You girls get settled and I will tend to the ice and start heating up the sauna."

Mo and Kirsti helped Rouva Aalto unload the groceries from the car. From the number of bags, it looked as if they had brought a smorgasbord with them.

"The food has already been cooked," Rouva Aalto said as she directed them into a large kitchen. "We'll just need to heat it up. Kirsti, could you set the table?"

Mo helped arrange *karjalan piirakka* and cardamom-spiced *pulla* bread on a couple of plates while Rouva Aalto heated several small casseroles in the microwave.

Herra Aalto returned just in time to eat, his clothes smudged with soot. "This one is a wood burner," he explained cheerfully. "It's the only true way to heat a sauna."

They ate a leisurely dinner as Herra Aalto trekked in and out of the cabin, stoking the sauna fire and checking the temperature. Finally, he announced that it was hot enough.

"You girls go ahead and take your turn." He pulled out his laptop. "We have some business to attend to first."

Kirsti led Mo down a snowy path to the small building, which Mo could now see sat right on the shore of a frozen lake. The sauna looked like a miniature log cabin on the outside, but the inside didn't look much different from the sauna back in the apartment building. The wood

fire added a smoky scent that mingled with the cedar.

They took their places on the benches and did the sweat-and-birch-branch thing. "So," Kirsti said, "did you learn what is *avanto* yet?"

Mo shook her head. She'd figured that maybe the word referred to the wood-burning kind of sauna, but judging by the sly smile on Kirsti's face, she was probably way, way off.

"*Avanto* means literally a hole in the ice."

Mo nodded, uncomprehending.

"*Avantouinti* is ice swimming. That is what we are going to do."

Mo's mouth dropped open. "What?"

"My father cut a hole in the ice on the lake," Kirsti said calmly. "Instead of rolling in the snow, we will jump into the water."

"You're kidding, right?"

"Not at all. This is a very traditional way to do sauna."

Right. Explain the weird stuff by calling it traditional. "But…what if you get stuck under the ice?"

"You won't. Just jump straight down and come straight back up. Let's go."

Kirsti threw open the door of the sauna and ran through the snow onto the frozen surface of the lake. Mo could see the dark shape of a hole in the ice, about four feet in diameter. Kirsti didn't slow down, but splashed feetfirst into the inky water. Mo hesitated, but only for a moment.

With a deep breath, she took a running leap for the hole in the ice.

The shock of the water would have made her scream out loud if the freezing blackness hadn't already closed over her head. She kicked and pushed upward, gasping as much from the cold as for breath when she surfaced. Kirsti was climbing out of the hole on a rope ladder. Mo swam quickly to the edge to do the same. Teeth chattering, she ran back into the sauna.

"Okay, that was really insane."

"But it felt good, didn't it?"

Mo had to admit that it did. And, she thought with a smile, now she had something to write home about in this week's e-mail.

Before practice on Monday, Coach Peltonen gathered the team together. "Before we begin this afternoon, we would like to welcome Jormo Aalto, president and owner of SkanTravel." He swept his hand, presenting their guest. "We owe SkanTravel our most sincere thanks for funding next week's trip to Kemi. Please give him a round of applause."

The group clapped and Herra Aalto waved his hands like a politician at a rally. "Please, please. It is my pleasure. Truly. We at SkanTravel admire you wonderful athletes. Sponsoring your trip and upcoming competition is an honor."

Mo couldn't help but notice that Kirsti hadn't joined in the clapping. In fact, she stood, arms folded, staring at the floor with her lips pressed together so tightly that they nearly disappeared.

Coach Peltonen's voice drew Mo's attention back to where he and Herra Aalto were standing. "SkanTravel has requested that we take some photographs of the group, so if you would please gather on this side of the room..."

When the team was assembled, a short man with a complicated-looking camera in his hands and a black leather bag hanging from his shoulder crouched before them and snapped a picture. The flash lit up the room and left negative spots of light in Mo's vision. She blinked and tried to focus.

He snapped several more pictures and then released the group. Mo had started to leave as well when the man gestured to her.

"*Paikalla*," he said, and pointed to a spot at Herra Aalto's side.

"He wants you to stand there," Riia whispered.

Mo nodded and took her place next to a beaming Herra Aalto. She couldn't help but notice that Kirsti hung back until the little man cornered her, too, and instructed her to stand front and center with her dad. The smile she affected for the picture disappeared as abruptly as the flash of the camera.

Mo stood uncomfortably, not knowing what to say.

"Um, thank you for arranging the trip, Herra Aalto. We're really looking forward to it."

"Not at all, not at all." He patted her on the shoulder then turned to the photographer and said something in Finnish. Kirsti stepped away, looking as if she had just bitten into a sour lingonberry.

Mo's heart dropped as the man smiled and raised his camera one more time. She forced a smile and posed with Kirsti's dad. She had understood only a few words of what he'd said, but they had been enough. "*Kip Clarkin tyttönsa.*" Kip Clark's daughter.

The cultural activity after practice that evening consisted of meeting in the library about the upcoming trip to northern Finland, so the local club members had to attend. Herra Aalto even put in an appearance. Much to Kirsti's dismay, he had announced the night before that he'd decided to accompany the club to Kemi as a chaperone. Rouva Aalto opted to stay behind. "Someone must keep an eye on the business," she'd said.

Herra Kolehmainen stood at the front of the room, fiddling with an old-fashioned overhead projector while Coach Peltonen set up a white screen.

Mo frowned as she took a seat next to Riia. Not much chance of it being a quick meeting if those two were tag-teaming. It was already six-thirty and she was supposed to meet with Leevi when they were through.

"What is wrong?" Riia whispered.

Before Mo could answer, Coach Peltonen clapped his hands. "All right, everyone. Listen up. We have a lot of material to go through tonight."

Mo sank deeper in her chair. Great.

"The trip to Kemi has two purposes," Coach Peltonen continued. "The first, of course, is for your cultural edification. The other is to enhance your cohesiveness as a team. We will be participating in several activities that will test your stamina and athletic abilities. I expect you to look out for each other. Work together. A unified team is a winning team."

He droned on about how jumping was both an individual sport and a team sport, but Mo was too busy watching the minutes tick away on the clock to pay much attention.

Finally, the coach turned the time over to Herra Kolehmainen, who dimmed the lights and switched on the overhead projector. An illuminated map image of Finland appeared on the screen. With a pencil as a shadowed pointer, he indicated a large body of water between Finland and Sweden. "This is the Gulf of Bothnia," he said. "Where we'll be going is right here." He tapped the map at the uppermost arch of the gulf. "This is Kemi. Notice how close it is to the Arctic Circle. Be prepared. It can be a bit colder up north."

Colder? Mo shivered just thinking about it. That is, until

she looked over her shoulder to find Leevi watching her. His eyes met hers and she felt warm all over. He pointed to his watch. Mo knit her brows and gave him a shrug. Yeah, she knew they were going to be late starting their "session," but what were they supposed to do, walk out on the meeting?

"Later," she mouthed.

He inclined his head, but the whole rest of the time, she could feel him looking at her, watching, waiting. Made it kind of hard to concentrate on what Herra Kolehmainen was saying.

The terrain was different up north. Check. Not as many lakes. Gotcha. Flats and fells. Whatever those are. Sámi people. What?

"The Sámi are indigenous people who live in the north-ernmost parts of Finland, Sweden, Norway, and Russia in an area widely known as Lappland," the coach said. "Please be aware, however, that the term *Lapp* is consid-ered derogatory by many Sámi nowdays."

Mo leaned close to Riia. "Are they the ones who herd reindeer?"

"Some of them," Riia whispered back.

"Will we get to see reindeer?"

"What do you think?"

Coach Peltonen shot them a pointed look and Mo straightened in her chair, trying to look contrite.

"The Sámi in Finland," Herra Kolehmainen continued,

"are Finnish citizens, but they have their own language, their own culture, and their own identity. As always, please be respectful while you are their guests."

When the session ended, Kirsti waited by the door as everyone filed out. Was she waiting for Mo? She never waited—or at least she hadn't for a long time. Why hadn't she left with her dad? Mo slid a glance over to where Leevi, too, was waiting. He wasn't being obvious about it; he just sat writing in his notebook. Mo hesitated. She didn't want to tell Kirsti she was meeting with Leevi, but she could hardly just walk out on him, either.

She approached Kirsti. "You can go on if you want. I'm going to swing by the *museo* before I head home."

Kirsti raised her brows. "For your project?"

"Um, yeah."

"I'll come with you. You can show me what you've been working on."

"Oh. I...uh, sure."

At that moment, Leevi stood and folded his tattered notebook and stuffed it inside his jacket. He walked out of the room without even a glance in Mo's direction. She didn't know whether to be relieved or hurt.

"All right," she said. "Let's go."

The whole time she and Kirsti were walking to the *museo,* Mo's mind was racing. How was she going to show Kirsti what she'd been working on when she hadn't been working on anything? Not for the report, anyway.

She hoped she was as good at bluffing as she'd gotten at lying.

They walked down a row of display cases until Mo saw something she recognized. The elite ski patrol! They'd talked about that in Finland class.

Mo stopped in front of the display and admired the pure white snowsuit. "I'm, um, studying about skiing in the Winter War right now," she said. "What I think is really cool is how you guys were able to defeat tanks with skis." She gave Kirsti a shaky smile.

Kirsti only raised a brow, looking unconvinced. "You could read about the ski patrol in a book. Why do you have to come here?"

"Um, I, um, like to get a visual for what I'm studying. When I learn about how the ski patrol camouflaged themselves against the snow by wearing white, I like to see the camouflage suits up close and personal. And, uh..." She quickly scanned the cases for another example. "When I learn about how the patrols were able to sneak right up to Russian tanks on their skis and throw a Molotov cocktail in the engine compartment of a tank, I like to know what a Molotov cocktail looks like." She pointed out a display of a bottle with a rag sticking out of it.

They walked through the *museo* a little longer and Mo was surprised to find how much she actually knew, just from browsing while she was waiting for the simulator. Good thing, since her paper was due in just a couple of weeks.

"You ready to go?" Mo asked. "I think I can work from home tonight." What she didn't say was that it might be a good time to actually get the report started.

Leevi seemed to be avoiding Mo in school the next day. Not like they normally hung out or anything, but now he seemed aloof, indifferent. She wasn't sure how she was supposed to react to that. Apologize for missing their workout the night before? Thank him for being discreet? Ignore him right back? That last one was much too hard. She settled on pretending that he wasn't being cool to her, smiling at him whenever she got the chance and trying not to let it hurt too much if he never smiled in return.

She pushed herself extra hard in practice, digging in during the cardio sprint race and leaving everyone else to eat her dust—or snow, as the case might be.

"That's what I like to see," Coach Peltonen said. "Now if you can take that energy with you up the hill, we should see some exceptional jumps from you today."

Leevi skied past her. "Pace yourself," he said in a low voice.

Well, at least he was talking to her.

That was enough to carry her to her best jump yet— eighty-two meters. Coach Peltonen applauded Mo as she slid to a stop at the top of the inrun, snow rooster-tailing behind her skis.

"There you go! You've got it!"

Great. Now she just hoped that she could keep it.

As the trip to Kemi neared, Mo began to feel the pressure. Between practice, completing her assignments, and preparing for the trip, she didn't have much left for her sessions with Leevi.

He watched her on the box jumps and shook his head. "Look, drills will only do so much. You've got to bring the rest."

"I am bringing it."

"Not even close."

"Hey, I jumped eighty-two from the K90 in practice tonight, did you see that? Eighty-two! And I nailed the style. With a performance like that, I can podium. We did it. Don't you think we can step it down a notch now?"

"Did it?" He lowered his brows. "You haven't jumped in the exhibition yet. And when did you decide eighty-two was the best you could do? What about when you fly from the *suurmäki*?"

"I'm happy with those numbers, okay? In fact, I'd say they're great, considering that I'm running on about three hours' sleep a night. What do you want from me?"

"I want you to focus. Stop acting like you've already crossed the finish line."

"Um, hate to tell ya, but there's no finish line in ski jumping."

Leevi settled his deep brown eyes on her. "Exactly. That

means there's no 'good enough.' No line you can cross that says the race is over, that you're done trying. You're going at it like this competition is your only goal. And what then? Are you done jumping or do you take it to the next level? What about that women's ski-jump event at the Olympics you keep talking about?"

Mo dropped onto the box. "Like that's going to happen. Look, this is the best I've ever done, and if you can't let me be proud of that, then—"

He folded his arms. "Be proud all you want, but keep moving forward. And yeah, you are good. Don't keep measuring yourself by everyone else."

"Well, if I measure myself by me, I'm doing better than I've ever done, so—"

He let out an exasperated growl. "You're not getting it. You can never reach the finish line, Clark. Not in your sport and not in your life. You come close, you set the line back. That way, you keep moving forward, keep getting better. When you think you're done, it's all over."

Mo's first inclination was to snap at him, but what he said made sense. She'd gotten better, and she could get better still. She stood and stepped onto the box. "Okay," she said, "I'm ready."

Chapter Eleven

The group left for Kemi Friday after school. With the traffic, the drive to the Helsinki airport took longer than the flight. It seemed that they had just leveled off and reached cruising altitude when they began their descent. Soon they were being herded through the small airport in Kemi and onto a bus bound for their hotel.

Coach Peltonen stood at the head of the bus as they drove along. "Please remember we are guests of SkanTravel while we are here and we must conduct ourselves accordingly. No wandering away from the group, no breaking curfew, no loud or obnoxious behavior…"

Mo slid a glance at Tapio and couldn't help but laugh to herself. He caught her eye and mouthed, "What?" She pressed her finger to her lips and turned her attention back to the coach. "You'll want to get your rest tonight," he said, "because we have a full day planned for you tomorrow." He held up a hideous red-orange thing that looked like the Michelin Man's second skin. "Each of you will be issued a thermal suit which should keep you warm and dry. Remember, these suits are your friends. Take care of them and they will take care of you."

The bus lumbered down an ice-rutted road until it reached an opening in the trees. In the clearing stood a two-story log building that Mo quickly learned was their hotel. It featured a rustic-looking wraparound porch populated by a collection of chisel-carved wooden bears.

They checked in to the hotel and ate dinner in shifts since the dining room could accommodate only twelve at a time. Herra Aalto volunteered to go last, which meant Mo and Kirsti waited for him as well. By the time they sat down to eat, it was pretty late. Most everyone else had already gone to bed by the time Kirsti and Mo reached their room.

Kirsti yawned. "I'm so tired I could drop right here."

"I'm wide awake," Mo said. "Probably 'cause we ate so late."

"You should try to go to sleep, though. We have an early start time in the morning."

Mo agreed. In fact, she did get ready for bed and tried to make herself go to sleep, but it wasn't working. The harder she tried, the more painfully she remained awake. She didn't know why she was so restless. After her intense week of preparation and practice, she really was exhausted. She wanted to sleep. She needed to sleep. She couldn't sleep.

From the lobby, the sound of the grandfather clock echoed down the halls. Twelve bongs. Midnight. Mo lay in the darkness and stared at the ceiling then rolled onto her side and stared at the shadowed wall. No good. She rolled onto her other side and stared at her thermal suit, draped across a chair. Could it really keep her as warm as Coach Peltonen claimed it would?

Only one way to find out.

She dressed quickly and slipped out of the room, tip-toeing down the hallway and back stairs to the lobby. If anyone from the group were down there—especially Coach Peltonen or Herra Aalto—she didn't know what she'd say. She was relieved to discover that she wouldn't have to find out. The lobby was deserted. She smiled at the desk clerk and let herself outside.

It was cold. Colder than it was in Lahti, probably, but once you hit twenty below, everything kinda feels the same. Mo pulled her knit hat down over her ears and adjusted her scarf so that it was covering her face. She crossed the porch and skipped down the steps. So far, so

good. The thermal suit felt warm enough, so she crunched over the snow to the field just beyond the soft glow of the hotel's welcome sign.

Her breath caught as she looked up to see bands of greenish light drifting across the midnight sky. The lights wavered, fading and growing brighter, as if God were playing with a giant movie projector. Streaks of red and blue rose and fell among the green, swirling and dancing.

"So, you like the aurora borealis?"

Mo startled and turned to find Leevi walking toward her. His face was shadowed and obscured by a fleece ski mask, but his eyes were clear and bright and watching her.

"I've never seen anything like it."

Leevi stepped closer and Mo trembled. "You cold?" he asked.

"Naw, I'm good." As soon as the words left her mouth, she cursed her stupidity. *No, doofus. Say you're cold! Let the guy warm you up.* "So...um...you're up late."

"Couldn't sleep. You?"

"Me, either."

He made a sound deep in his throat but said nothing further. She turned back to the lights and he watched the sky with her in companionable silence. The random undulations were hypnotizing. Spellbinding. Soon everything else faded away but the two of them and the magnetism of electrons and ions crackling overhead. When he edged nearer, so that his chin was almost resting on her head, it felt like the most natural thing in the world. So natural that she leaned into him without thinking, drawing on the warmth of his contact, the comfort in his presence.

"Listen," he said quietly. "Do you hear it?" His voice broke the spell and all of a sudden she was very conscious of their proximity.

"Hear what?" she managed to whisper.

"This. The electricity." He swept his arm toward the sky and she followed the motion, turning her head until she found his cheek next to hers. She held her breath. "The Sámi call it *guovssahas*. A light that can be heard."

"I can't hear it," she whispered.

"Listen harder." He slipped his arm around her waist and they stood motionless. Mo wanted to hear what he was talking about, she really did, but her brain was already on overload. All she could process was one sensation at a time. Like the feel of him pressed close against her back. His clean guy smell—soap and leather and the tang of damp wool. The noise of her own heart beating out a rumba in her chest.

"Wait. Is it that kind of like static in the air?"

She could feel his head nodding against hers. "The ancients believed the northern lights held special power." His voice rumbled low in her ear. "The Finns call the lights *revontulet*, which means 'fox fire.' They say it comes from a Sámi legend about a fox's tail swatting snow into the sky.

But the old language had another word that sounds like the word for fox. It means magic. The Finns got it wrong. This was meant to be called magic fire." He paused for a moment. "Do you feel it?"

Mo twisted around to face him. Magic? Absolutely. Sparks were flying like the Fourth of July.

His eyes locked on hers as he pulled the fleece of his mask below his chin. Her fingers trembled as she did the same with her scarf. Despite the cold, her face burned hot, then hotter still as he cupped the back of her head in his hand and pulled her closer.

She could barely breathe when his lips touched hers. She closed her eyes and felt as if she were flying without skis.

"So there you are!" Kirsti's voice raked through the air like steel on ice.

Leevi pulled away, cold clamping Mo where his body had been. She wanted to cry. "Kirsti. I didn't know you were up."

"I see," Kirsti said, those two small words carrying an impressively large load of innuendo. "When I noticed your bed was empty, I got worried. It's way past curfew."

Guilt clamped down on top of the cold. "Oh. Yeah. I couldn't sleep, so I thought I'd go for a walk. The lights..." She waved weakly skyward, but the enchantment was gone. All that remained of the northern lights was a faint green glow near the horizon. As for the magic that had cocooned her and Leevi, that seemed to be gone, too. He stood stiffly at her side and Mo couldn't help but notice that Kirsti hadn't even acknowledged he was there. He returned the snub with cool detachment. "I guess I should go in now," Mo said, though neither one of them seemed to hear her.

Chapter Twelve

Mo woke before the sun, which, with only six hours of light this time of year, wasn't much of a trick. Her chest felt tight, like when she had forgotten something important or messed up in a competition. What happened last night? Had she really kissed Leevi? She got dizzy just thinking about it.

The thought that she had been playing with fire niggled in the darkened fringes of Mo's mind. She really liked Leevi, but this...whatever it was, went against everything she had ever been taught. It was never a good idea for clubmates to get involved. Her dad always said it to his athletes and her coach had said the same thing to her.

But...did that really apply to Leevi? The circumstances were way different from what her coach was talking about, and besides, they would be on totally separate continents in just a few weeks—not that the thought did anything to lift her spirits. But did that make it okay?

Falling for Leevi had definitely not been part of the plan, but she was falling just the same. The question was, should she enjoy the plunge or grab on to the nearest ledge and hold on for dear life?

Mo showered and pulled on her ever-stylish thermal suit. In the mirror, she looked like a big orange blob. Just the look she was going for.

Kirsti had been quiet all morning, speaking in monosyllables and avoiding eye contact. Mo wasn't quite sure if Kirsti was angry or hurt, but she got the message loud and clear that Kirsti was unhappy with her.

"I'm sorry," she said for about the tenth time that morning. "I shouldn't have snuck out."

Kirsti finally responded, turning away from her book long enough to glare at Mo. "Do you know what it means for my parents to sponsor a trip like this? It means they accept responsibility for the participants. Your little rendezvous could have damaged their reputation, did you think of that?"

"It wasn't a rendezvous. We didn't plan anything. I just went for a walk and Leevi—" She stopped. "Look, I'm sorry. You're right. I wasn't thinking."

Kirsti turned away. "We should go down now. Everyone will be waiting."

Mo's heart clunked unpleasantly as they descended the stairs. Leevi would be down there and she wasn't ready to face him yet. What would she say to him? How would she act? Now might be a good time to keep her distance. At least until she had a chance to figure things out.

Coach Peltonen looked up from his clipboard as Mo and Kirsti reached the lobby. "Ah, there we go. All present and accounted for."

Everyone in the club turned, seemingly in unison, to stare at them. Nothing like making an entrance. Mo shrugged and offered up an apologetic smile. Leevi caught her eye from the back corner and grinned. She started to smile back but quickly dropped her gaze.

"Let's get started!" Coach Peltonen rubbed his hands eagerly. "We've got a lot to see today." A wave of glacial air swept into the room as he opened the door, barely cooling the fire in Mo's face. She slipped out ahead of the group, pulling her hat down over her ears.

In the pale morning light, Mo hid behind her sunglasses and tried to act interested in the line of snowmobiles waiting in front of the hotel. She saw Leevi step outside, pulling up his ski mask as he went. She edged farther away and only half listened as the tour guide gave instructions and reviewed a list of safety precautions.

"Now, then," he said. "Choose a partner to ride with and let's go."

Mo didn't want to take the chance that Leevi would ask her to be his partner. Or that he wouldn't. She turned to grab the closest person she could. That person just happened to be Kirsti. "Let's call a truce and ride together, okay? We can—"

"I have to go with my dad. Why don't you ride with Tapio or someone?" She gestured toward the lineup of guys. Several of them were arguing over who had to sit on the back of the snowmobiles and who got to drive. In their matching thermal suits and helmets they looked like bad-tempered clones.

Tapio waved from astride a shiny black Polaris and Mo ran to join him. He revved the engine as she secured her helmet. Boys and their toys.

She had barely swung her leg over the back and settled onto the seat when he yelled above the noise. "Hold on!"

"What?"

The snowmobile leaped forward and Mo wrapped her arms around Tapio's waist. Soon they were racing over the rippled white ice fields, wind rushing over them like water, whipping Tapio's exhilarated yell behind him. Mo laughed and let the joy of the moment take over. Fun now, worry later.

Not long after they set out, the mist burned off to reveal a cobalt sky. Crystal snow flashed and sparkled in the sunlight. It was perfect, Mo thought, or would be, if... Her thoughts drifted to Leevi once again and she flinched. Tapio patted her hand reassuringly. Mo grimaced. If he only knew.

On the other edge of the ice flats, snow-shrouded trees pointed to the sky. Many of the trunks were bent and twisted from years of wind and snow as they wound their way upward, giving the forest a fantasy touch. The guide slowed and directed each of them to follow, single file, along a narrow path through the trees.

Too soon the ride was over and they came upon the camp. Teams of sled dogs and even a small herd of reindeer clustered in a large clearing dotted with wooden tepees and cabins. Camp workers dressed in colorful Sámi costumes waved and directed the snowmobilers to where they could park their machines.

Tapio inched the Polaris to its designated spot and killed the engine. Mo crawled from the back and pulled off her helmet.

"Woo-hoo! That was wicked!"

"Kyllä sikamakee!" Tapio pulled off his helmet.

Mo's smile faded. It wasn't Tapio at all, but Leevi grinning back at her. She stumbled.

Leevi reached out to steady her. "Whoa. Better give yourself a minute to get your land legs."

At his touch, Mo's heart dropped right into her boots. And she'd been riding all morning with her arms wrapped around his waist! Heat washed over her face and she pulled away. "I'm good. Thanks." She shifted the helmet awkwardly in her hands, unable to meet his eye. She should talk to him, she knew, but she didn't know what to say. "Um, thanks." She placed the helmet on the seat and backed away, thumbing vaguely over her shoulder. "I've got to go, uh…"

He looked confused.

"I'll see you," she said, and escaped.

Riia and the real Tapio stood near a large fire pit in the center of the clearing where the group was gathering. Mo rushed toward them.

"Wasn't that great?" Riia gushed.

Mo could only nod as Leevi approached the group, brows pinched, eyes scanning faces. She turned her head and feigned interest in whatever it was Tapio was saying. To be honest, she hadn't heard a word. Her head was too full of her own words—questions and thoughts flying back and forth at such speed, there was no way she could pin one down long enough to examine it.

What exactly was her problem? Running from Leevi wasn't going to solve anything, but she just couldn't deal with him right now. Not until she got a grip on the situation. On her feelings. Leevi was a friend. She'd be wise to keep it that way. Right?

It was too much to think about right now. Mo turned her attention to the man laughing with Coach Peltonen on the other side of the fire. If he wasn't a good distraction, she didn't know what was. From head to toe, the man was dressed in a vivid array of blues and reds and yellows. His hat looked like a court jester's, the crown divided into four drooping points. Colorful woven ribbons encircled the brim and hung to his shoulders in the back. Bright patterns similarly decorated the shoulders, collar, cuffs, and hem of his blue wool tunic, which he wore belted at the waist over darker blue trousers. He slapped one mittened hand on Coach Peltonen's shoulder and the two men turned to admire the nearest pack of huskies. As they stepped away from the fire, Mo almost laughed out loud at the curling toes of the man's boots. That little touch brought to mind some kind of Nordic genie.

Mo wandered over to the nearest sled team once the men had moved on.

The dogs eyed her as she approached, placid expressions unchanging. They were probably well accustomed to tourists. One bundled-up human must look pretty much the same as any other. She advanced with caution anyway, reaching out a hand to let the lead dog sniff it. He wagged his tail and nudged her fingers with his nose.

"Oh, you like this, do you?" She dropped to one knee and stroked his head. The other dogs pressed in, yipping, tails slapping back and forth like furry windshield wipers.

"Looks like they all want to get in on the attention." It was Leevi. His face was hidden behind his ski mask, but Mo could hear the smile in his voice. He knelt next to her, caressing fur, cooing to the dogs.

Mo shifted uncomfortably.

"Beautiful, aren't they?" he said.

Mo nodded and ran her hand over a muscular back, down one powerful flank. The dog watched her with other-worldly blue eyes—wild eyes. "This one looks like a wolf."

"Wouldn't doubt it. Some are all husky, but many are at least half wolf. He likes you, that's for sure. Looks like we've found our team."

"What?"

"Our dog team, for when we drive the sleds."

But that's not what Mo was asking. She was still stuck on the word *our*. How was she supposed to clear her head with him throwing stuff like that at her?

"Uh, I...I'm sorry." Mo stood. "I told Tapio I'd go with him."

Leevi's hands stilled. "Oh."

Leaving Leevi with the dogs, Mo retreated back to the fire where Tapio was talking with a group of guys.

"Tapio! There you are. You want to drive a team with me?"

Too late, Mo noticed Riia standing nearby. She tried to ignore the stricken look on Riia's face when Tapio grinned and said, "Sure. You find a favorite?"

Mo looked to where Leevi continued talking with the dogs. Saw how they responded to him, tails wagging, gathering around him like he was one of their own. He was a lot like them…beautiful. Wild. She swallowed a lump in her throat. "Not really."

"I like that team there." Tapio took her arm. "Let's go have a look."

A short time later, Herra Kolehmainen, Coach Peltonen, and the Sámi guide returned to the fire pit and gathered the group together for some quick instructions.

"Don't forget to record this experience in your *Suomen päiväkirja*," Herra Kolehmainen reminded them, and then turned the time over to the guide.

"Divide up," the man said, "two men to a team; one musher and one passenger. We will have a resting period at midday and you can switch then if you desire."

"I call first," Mo whispered to Tapio.

He shook his head. "No way."

"Way."

"I'll arm-wrestle you for it."

"Ha. Rock, paper, scissors."

"*Kivi, sakset, paperi?* You're on."

Coach Peltonen shot them a look. Mo mouthed "sorry" and turned her attention back to the guide, hoping that she hadn't missed any vital information.

As it was, start time was crazy anyway, so even if she had been listening, it might not have helped. The moment the dogs were harnessed to the sled, they began barking and jumping and pulling on the lead.

"They can't wait to get started," Tapio shouted.

"What?"

"Let's do it!"

Mo won at *kivi, sakset, paperi* and Tapio settled into the sledge's seat, scowling.

As she familiarized herself with the sled and located the brakes—one silver one rimmed with little teeth, and one rubber pad—several of the dogs took a break from their yapping and squatted down to poop in the snow.

"Oh, that's vile." Mo tapped Tapio on the shoulder. "You wanna help me clean that up?"

"You're the musher, you clean it." He settled back in his fur-lined seat, his scowl replaced with a smug smile.

"Just bury it," the guide said. Mo's face must have betrayed her disbelief because he laughed. "Really. It's fine."

Mo gingerly kicked snow on top of the steaming piles, hoping she wouldn't unearth any other buried treasures in the process. "Why do they all have to do this together?" she grumbled. "What is it, a team sport?"

"They are preparing themselves. The dogs love the run, but it is hard work. They are also testing you. You must show them you are the alpha. Start with Kaira. He is the lead dog. The others will do as he does."

Mo looked helplessly at Tapio. What was she supposed

to do, growl? Make a mean face? Tapio just chuckled. Some help. She didn't have much time to worry about it, though, because the first sleds were already taking to the trail and the dogs began straining at the lead.

"Kaira!" Mo yelled over the din. "Um... settle down!"

She could just imagine the dogs laughing at her as she rushed to the back of the sled. As she'd been instructed, she placed one foot on a runner, held on to the sled tightly with one hand, and reached out to undo the slipknot on the tie-rope with the other. Either the tie-rope was frozen or the knot wasn't of the slip variety because the thing wouldn't budge. She was still tied to the tree and all of the other sleds were gliding down the trail.

Panicked, Mo let go of the sled and wrestled the knot with both hands. When the thing slipped free, the dogs bolted. She had to sprint to catch up. Time and again she reached out to grab hold of the handles to pull herself on, but the sled bumped or swerved and she couldn't reach it. The dogs picked up speed and she lost ground. One of the guides had to cut in front of her team to head them off. He yelled something to Kaira in a language that sounded similar yet somehow different from Finnish, and the dogs slowed. Mo managed to catch up to the sled only to be rewarded by Tapio's laughter ringing in her ears. The turd. She jumped onto the runners and shouted to the dogs and they were off again. Oh, yeah. This was going to make a great entry in her *päiväkirja*.

The first thing that Mo realized about dogsledding, besides the fact that one should hold on to the sled when the tie-rope is released, was that it really didn't take much effort to drive. Not with these dogs, anyway. They knew what to do and where to go—follow the lead sled. Her only challenge, once she had finally gotten on the sled, was to not fall off.

She stood on the back runners, concentrating to keep her balance. When the dogs cornered, she cornered with them, crouching to keep her center of gravity low and leaning her weight on the inside runner. It was a good workout, but not really that difficult. Before long she managed to relax the tension in her neck, shoulders, and arms and let herself move with the sled.

They plunged into a forest of gingerbread-iced trees, the trail winding and curving, dipping and climbing. The dogs were silent, intent on the run. The only sounds Mo could hear were their panting breaths and the hiss of the sled's runners through the snow.

She closed her eyes and lifted her face to both the wind and the hazy winter sun and let her mind empty. This was freedom, pure and simple. She wished the moment could go on forever.

Of course, the instant she opened her eyes she was thrust back into reality; just ahead, Leevi curved in front of her, driving his team like a pro, riding the bumps and curves with fluid motion. Her chest tugged as she watched

him go, and she wished…she wished…She wished she wasn't so confused.

Just before noon, they reached another clearing. The savory aroma of cooking meat filled the air and Mo's stomach rumbled as she stood on the foot brake, bringing her team to a stop. She looked around hungrily and saw another Sámi guide stirring a big black pot over an open fire.

"Lunch!" Tapio said as he unfolded himself from the seat of the sled. "Come on!"

Mo tied the lead to a tree and hurried behind Tapio to where the group was gathering.

"You are hungry?" the guide asked. "So how do you think the dogs feel, eh? They have done all the work." He uncovered a huge pile of brownish-red meat chunks. "First you see to your teams. Then we'll talk about lunch."

As the musher, Mo hauled their portion to the dogs. The team's wild side took over almost before the food was set down. They growled and clawed and ripped at the meat and Mo jumped back, trembling.

"You can't lose control," a voice behind her said. Mo didn't even have to turn around to know it was Leevi. If only he knew. He stepped up beside her. "They won't see you as the alpha if you act timid."

She looked up at him. "I'm not strong enough to not be timid," she said. And she wasn't talking about the dogs.

• • •

Later that afternoon, Herra Kolehmainen stood at the head of the dimly lit bus and raised his voice over the rumble of the motor. "I know we are all exhausted from today's excursion, but you'll want to stay alert for our next stop. We'll be visiting the famous *LumiLinna*. That means 'snow castle,' for those of you who haven't done your reading yet, and it is built entirely from snow and ice."

He kept talking, but Mo tuned him out. She glanced over her shoulder, looking for Riia, who had not come to sit by Mo on this ride as she usually would. Not that Mo blamed her. Before the day was through, she was going to have to make things right with Riia. And with Tapio, who, she had to admit, she had soundly used. She sighed and slouched down in her seat.

Lunch still sat like a lump of ski wax in her stomach. And not even because she'd found out halfway through the meal that what they were eating was reindeer. No, it probably had more to do with the fact that she couldn't get the thing with Leevi out of her head.

The bus turned from the main street and crunched over the ice in a wide parking area. Ahead of them, bright lights illuminated the battlements, towers, and turrets of a stark white castle, complete with snowy archway and a drawbridge.

Mo leaned toward the aisle so she could get a better look through the bus's windshield. What caught her attention was Leevi's profile as he watched out the window, just

a few seats ahead of her, his hair all tousled from sleep. Shadow and light skated across his face as the bus passed under a streetlamp. The effect painted his features first vulnerable, then mysterious. Mo eased back into her seat, stomach doing the helium thing. No denying it. She... really... liked... him. Why should she let some stupid self-imposed rule keep her from letting him know?

She shouldn't. The decision came so quickly, she bolted up in her seat. She would tell him. Now. She stood, but the bus lurched to a stop and she fell back down. Before she could recover, everyone else started getting up and crowding the aisle. She lost sight of Leevi as he climbed from the bus with Coach Peltonen.

By the time Mo got off the bus, the group was gathering around the Snow Castle guide—a man in a white parka who was holding a blue flag high above his head.

"*Tervetuloa,*" the guide said in a loud voice. "Welcome to *LumiLinna*. How many of you have been here before?" Only Herra Aalto raised his hand. "Well, then, it looks like I have a lot to show you."

He ushered the group over the snow drawbridge and through the arched snow entryway into a packed-snow courtyard. After a quick tour of the snow and ice buildings in the compound, including a chapel, a hotel, and an icy labyrinth, Coach Peltonen turned the group loose to explore. "We will go in to dinner at seven o'clock. You are to meet in this spot by quarter of. Understood? Good. Now enjoy!"

Mo looked for Leevi. She didn't see him, but she did see Riia. She chewed her lip. As much as she wanted to go looking for Leevi, she owed Riia an apology and she shouldn't put it off. Mo called to her, but Riia either didn't hear or pretended not to.

Tapio stepped up next to Mo. "What's with her tonight?"

"Nothing."

"Nothing? I just asked her if she wanted to see the ice maze and she looked like she was going to hit me."

Mo kicked at the snow. "It's not you. She's kind of upset with me."

"*Eiks niin?* So what's the drama about?"

Mo spoke without thinking. "You." She clapped her hand over her mouth and shook her head, but it was too late.

He laughed. "Oh, yes, of course. That I can understand. I have women fighting over me all the time."

"I'm so not fighting."

"And she is?"

Mo drew an exasperated breath. "Look, I wasn't even supposed to let you know she's interested, okay? Just—"

"She's interested? In me?" His smile faded. "Are you being serious?"

She nodded gravely.

"She *likes* me?" He turned a speculative gaze to where Riia was standing.

Mo nodded again.

The transformation on his face said it all. First came surprise, then contemplation, perhaps a little speculation, and then genuine pleasure. "Really? How do you know?"

"How do you *not* know?"

"She never said anything."

"Oh, come on. Like she's going to tell you."

"Why not? Wouldn't that make things a whole lot easier?"

Mo blew out a breath. "Well, sure, for you. All you have to do is sit back and let her declare her undying devotion. But what if you don't like her back? Then she's going to feel completely—"

"Undying devotion, huh?"

"Would you just listen to me?"

"So what does this have to do with you?"

"Well..." Mo hesitated. This was going to be harder than she thought. How did she explain without sounding like a total slime? She couldn't. She had been a slime. "I...I kind of asked you to drive the sled team with me even though I knew she liked you."

"Hey, she has no claim on me. Just because—"

"Oh, stop it. We both know you like her, too."

His smile broadened. "It shows?"

"Um, yeah."

"So she's jealous?"

"You really need to get over yourself." She slugged his arm. It was then she finally saw Leevi—across the compound, watching them.

Oh, crud. She could imagine what this must look like. After the sled thing, all she needed was for Leevi to think she was after Tapio.

And that's when she saw Riia on the other side, also watching, the hurt in her eyes turning cold.

"You better go talk to her," Mo said. "I need to, uh..." She glanced back to where Leevi had been standing, but he was gone.

Chapter Thirteen

That night, dinner was held in a snow dining hall furnished with long ice tables and ice-block seats topped with reindeer pelts. Ice goblets sat at each place and intricate ice sculptures served as centerpieces. The group appropriately oohed and ahhed and then moved into the room, sitting in clusters around the tables. Mo never did find Leevi again out in the compound, so she hoped she would be able to corner him during dinner.

That is, until Herra Aalto insisted that Herra Kolehmainen, Coach Peltonen, Kirsti, and Mo sit with him at the center table. She watched helplessly as Leevi entered the room and took a seat far away from where she would be.

"The meal will be served buffet style," Herra Aalto said. "You'll find a delectable variety of traditional Finnish dishes." Then, lowering his voice, he leaned toward Kirsti. "Some of the stews tend to be rather rich, so you will want to avoid them. Can't have you putting on weight just before the competition."

Kirsti frowned and looked to her lap, but Herra Aalto seemed not to notice. He droned on about the types of food he'd sampled at *LumiLinna* with past tour groups. Coach Peltonen nodded politely even though Mo noticed his eyes strayed more than once.

Finally, a bearded man in a blue and red tunic stepped into the room and announced that the group could proceed to the buffet table. Herra Aalto stood and clapped a hand on Coach Peltonen's shoulder. "After you, Arho."

Mo followed them to the buffet and looked over the assortment of rich stews and casseroles, wrinkling her nose. Were they kidding? Reindeer stew, smoked reindeer roast, reindeer sausage, reindeer fry. Suddenly she lost her appetite.

Coach Peltonen nudged her arm. "You need to eat," he said. She obediently dished up a cup of white-fish soup and a couple of smoked salmon sandwiches on rye flatbread even though she didn't think she'd touch them.

Back at the table, Mo picked at her food and tried not to look too bored while Herra Aalto, Herra Kolehmainen,

and Coach Peltonen yammered away in rapid Finnish. Kirsti didn't look any more interested even though she could actually understand what they were saying.

As inconspicuously as she could, Mo scanned the room, looking for Leevi. She saw Tapio and Riia sitting at a table together, heads bent close as they laughed about something. A little pang of jealousy stabbed, although she really was happy for them. And with luck, the positive outcome would help Riia forgive Mo for being such an idiot.

Finally, she spotted Leevi, sitting with the Canadian guys near the back of the room. She willed him to make eye contact, but he seemed to be consciously avoiding looking anywhere near her direction. She slumped in her seat. Okay, so maybe after dinner then.

As the meal wound to a close, Herra Aalto stood and tapped his ice goblet with a spoon. It made kind of a weird *ploing, ploing, ploing* sound, but it was enough to get everyone to quiet down. "May I have your attention, please? The bus will arrive to transport us back to the hotel in less than an hour. Those who would like to take a quick peek at the sleeping quarters of *LumiLinna*, please finish up quickly. We will meet in the lobby in ten minutes."

Mo's shoulders drooped. At this rate, she was never going to be able to talk to Leevi.

The bedroom-tour group met the guide in the hotel lobby, where an elaborate ice sculpture glowed softly in the center of the room. Off to one side of the lobby,

174

patrons crowded into an ice bar, talking and laughing and drinking Finlandia vodka, according to the sign on the wall, in little ice shot glasses.

As the guide gushed about the features of the hotel, Mo fidgeted and glanced over her shoulder. She drew in a sharp breath. Leevi was standing directly behind her, at the back of the group. She started to turn around.

"Mo!" Kirsti hissed. "Come on."

Mo reluctantly followed Kirsti as the guide led them along an icy corridor. Torchlike sconces hung from iron rings embedded in the walls, lighting the way.

"Each room can accommodate four guests," the guide said. He opened the door to one of the sleeping rooms and Mo shuddered. The place reminded her of a morgue; each "bed" was a table of ice where she imagined dead bodies might be laid out. "You may notice that, for obvious reasons, the rooms are not equipped with plumbing," he continued, "We advise our guests to use the WC before bedding down for the night or they may find themselves taking a rather chilly midnight stroll."

A hot blush crept across Mo's cheeks as she remembered her own midnight stroll the night before. She glanced back at Leevi. Would there be another meeting with him under the stars? He finally met her eye, but the look he gave her was guarded. She wanted to talk to him right then, but with Kirsti standing by her side, the best she could hope for was that he understood her smile.

• • •

Later that night, Mo lay in her bed at the main hotel, staring at the glowing red numbers on the clock. Though it was nearly midnight, Kirsti was still awake; Mo could tell by the way she was breathing—deep and deliberate. No way was Mo going to be able to sneak outside without Kirsti knowing. Even if she did, there was no guarantee Leevi would be there. Not after the way she'd acted all day.

In the morning she'd make things right. All she needed was a chance to talk to him. She touched her fingers to her lips. Well, she could dream, anyway.

When she awoke, Mo showered and dressed in record time. She packed quickly, rolled her suitcase down to the lobby, and set out to look for Leevi.

It wasn't long before she found him, only not exactly the way she had planned.

He came at her with fire in his eyes the moment she stepped out onto the front porch. "You're really a piece of work, you know that?"

Mo was so surprised by the aggression that she took a step back. So he was upset about the way she'd acted. But, wow. His anger seemed a little disproportionate. Still, she tried to apologize. "Look, I'm sorry about yesterday. I was—"

"Yeah, I know what you were. I just wouldn't have expected it from you."

"What are you talking about?"

"You heard me. You act all self-righteous, preaching against discrimination, but you're just as bad as anyone else. In fact, you're worse because you're a hypocrite as well as a bigot. Well, if you're too good for me, you're too good for my help. The deal is off."

With that, he stormed away. Mo could only stare after him. Part of her wanted to run after him and explain how he had it all wrong, but the other part of her wanted to slap him on the face. Who did he think he was, anyway, attacking her like that? If he wasn't willing to give her the benefit of the doubt, she certainly wasn't going to go begging for his forgiveness.

It was then she noticed Kirsti standing on the opposite end of the porch. Even though she appeared to be lost in her own world, looking out over the frozen, white landscape, Mo had a feeling she had heard every word.

Mo set her cell phone's alarm for three in the morning and put the phone under her pillow. It probably wouldn't be necessary; she hadn't done much sleeping since she'd gotten back from Kemi. Every night her mind kept replaying scenes from the weekend like a bad melodrama in off-season reruns. Three nights of that was more than enough.

As she had expected, she drifted in and out most of the night but was wide awake when the alarm beeped.

She quickly switched it off and lay very still, listening for any movement from the other side of the room. Carefully, quietly, she slid out from under her heavy comforter and tiptoed to the door.

In the living room, she sat on the couch and pressed the phone to her ear, waiting for Nessa to answer.

"Mo?"

"It's me."

"What is it? What's happened?"

Mo let the story tumble out. "And now Leevi hasn't spoken to me for three days. He won't even look at me. At first I felt really bad, but now it's starting to tick me off. I mean, I apologized for what I did. What more does he want? And Riia! I can't believe she got so upset when I told Tapio how she felt about him."

"Well..." Nessa drew out the word. "You did promise her you wouldn't say anything."

"Yeah, but I was trying to..." She blew out a breath. "No. You're right. I'd probably kill you if you told some guy I was crushing on him."

"Thank you for that."

"You know what I mean. At least she got over it, so we can still be friends. Of course, I think it helps that Tapio likes her back and they're the new cute couple in the school."

"So much for not dating clubmates."

"Yeah. Hellooo?"

"And what about your roomie?"

"Kirsti has been really weird. Like, not real cold, but not exactly friendly, either. She doesn't seem mad anymore, so I don't know what it is with her. This whole place has turned into the Twilight Zone."

"So what are you going to do?"

Mo fingered the piping on the couch. "What can I do? I'm going to work my butt off to get to the games. Without anybody's help."

Which, she realized, is why she had wanted to come to Finland in the first place.

Mo hung back the next evening after practice until most of her clubmates had gone, and then ducked into the museum building. The lady at the front desk who collected the entry fee gave her a friendly smile. It had been a while since she'd had been to the *museo*, but she had obviously been remembered.

She was on her own now; no Leevi to push her along. With the exhibition just a few days away, she'd had to come up with something to fill the void, so here she was.

As she waited for a turn on the jump simulator, she pulled out her math book and waded through her homework, graphing trigonometric functions. As soon as the simulator was free, she scrambled inside. It felt weird being back again. She glanced over her shoulder, half expecting Leevi to be standing there with that annoying

grin on his face. But, of course, Leevi wasn't anywhere to be seen.

After virtually jumping only a few times, Mo stepped out of the booth. She was too depressed to continue. Sure, the computer confirmed what she had seen on the hills; her jump distance had improved considerably. At least the time she had spent with Leevi had been worth something.

She moped around the museum for a while, but it wasn't doing anything for her mood. See? This was exactly why she shouldn't have let herself get attached to him. It hurt too much. The hopeful thoughts that had been dancing through her head scattered like cockroaches confronted by light. Whatever she had thought had been happening between her and Leevi obviously hadn't been. Time to face the fact and move on. Things were what they were.

On her way to the door, she walked past the white snowsuit in the ski patrol display and she slowed, trailing her fingers on the glass.

Sisu.

She'd learned by now the kind of "deal with it" attitude that came with *sisu*. That's what the Finnish army had to have in order to take on an enemy over twice its strength—what the Elite Ski Patrol had to have to sneak up on tanks and enemy encampments. And it was what she was going to have to develop if she was going to make it through these last couple of weeks.

Sisu. Perseverance. Stubbornness.

She stared at the display. The Finns were never ones to sit around and cry when things got tough. They just got tougher. In a land that was bitter cold and snow-locked half the year, they didn't whine about it; they went out and made things to put on their feet so they could get around. Only a people who really had *sisu* could make a game out of a part of life that had been created to deal with hardship.

She straightened. Well, she wasn't going to hang around feeling sorry for herself, either. She had finals coming up and her paper due in the Finland class and a competition to prepare for and that's what she was going to do. *Sisu?* Yeah, she had that.

Chapter Fourteen

It had taken three solid days of work, compiling her notes, checking her sources, making sure her Finland paper was complete, but she had done it! Good thing, since it was due the next day. She leaned back in her chair and admired her work. Once she'd gotten into it, it really hadn't been that bad. In fact, she had really enjoyed learning about skiing in Finland. It actually made her appreciate her sport more.

Kirsti was studying on her bed. Mo didn't want to interrupt her, but this was a major deal for her; it was the last hurdle to cross before the exhibition on Thursday.

"I finished," she said.

Kirsti looked up. "Huh?"

"My paper." She pointed to the computer monitor. "All I have to do is print it out and I'm done!"

Kirsti looked unimpressed. "Good." She went back to her studying.

Mo deflated. Well, she had to tell *someone* her good news. She stared at the blinking cursor for a moment, then signed on to the Internet.

To: kclark@email.com
From: mntmojo@email.com
Subject: Weekly Report

Hei from Finland!

Only two more days until the games. Woo-hooo!

I just finished a report on the history of skiing in Finland and I thought maybe you especially, Dad, would be interested in some of the stuff I learned.

Like, the oldest known ski was found in a peat bog and dates back over four thousand years, but Finns believe skiing goes back even further than that. (There's a story in the Kalevala that's supposed to have taken place when the world was first created when one of the heroes goes out to hunt and they say he skied so fast that his ski pole smoked in the snow. Sounds like someone I know. ☺)

But what I think is really cool is that all this history leads up to what I'm going to be doing on Thursday. No matter

how I do in the competition, I am going to be part of that history.

Thanks, Mom and Dad, for letting me come. I wouldn't trade this experience for anything in the world.

I love you.

Mo

Thursday arrived with a cold front and the threat of snow. Mo watched anxiously out the car window as Herra Aalto drove her and Kirsti to the Sports Center.

"Not to worry," he said. "We've held the Games in a blizzard before. Even worse is when the spring comes early and the snow is too soft for racing. This is nothing."

Mo nodded. Intellectually she understood what he was saying, but inside... inside she was tied in knots. She and Kirsti changed and met the others in the wax room to prepare their skis.

Mo paced back and forth as they waited their turn, shivering and rubbing her arms. Despite the kerosene heater, she felt cold down to her bones—and it wasn't from the temperature, either.

She closed her eyes and made herself take a deep breath. Just beyond the walls of the wax room, the stands were completely filled with spectators. Spectators who were there to watch her jump. Her stomach felt queasy. She was no stranger to competitions, but none of the

184

Juniors events had ever drawn the kinds of crowds she was seeing today. Even the Continental Cup in Park City drew only a fraction of these people. According to Herra Aalto, tens of thousands of people filled the stadium, and she'd seen camera crews prowling the area who would no doubt broadcast it to thousands—no, millions—more.

Of course, Mo knew that her exhibition wasn't the big draw. The Nordic sprint training run was enough to bring in a crowd. But the fact was, all those people were out there, and they would be watching.

"We're up," Coach Peltonen said. His voice seemed very far away. Mo shouldered her skis and fell in line with the other girls as they made their way to the lift that would take them to the bottom of the *suurmäki* big hill. This was it. The moment she had been waiting for since she'd first heard about the SAE program. The moment she had worked for, sacrificed for. The moment that was going to make everything that went before worth the pain.

And she was ready.

They walked past where Mo knew the guys would be standing among the spectators. She tried not to look, but she couldn't help herself. Sure enough, there they were... all except Leevi, that is. She allowed a little disappointment, but hardened herself against anything more. The only thing she could worry about for the moment were her jumps. Everything else could come later.

As she rode the elevator up to the top, she tried to visualize a perfect jump. One hundred ten, one hundred fifteen meters. Sure. Why not? Perfect form. Elegant landing. Leevi waiting at the top of the outrun...

She shook her head free of that last image.

"What's the matter?" Riia whispered.

"Nothing. Everything's fine."

After the first three girls had jumped, it was clear that everything was not fine. The weather wasn't working in their favor. Steel-gray clouds hung low, threatening snow, and a tailwind gusted strong enough to cause control issues. Mo squared her shoulders. No problem. She could adjust for that...just as long as it didn't change direction or get too strong.

The wind died down for a moment and the fourth jumper was able to control her form, earning better style marks than the first three jumpers.

Kirsti was number five. She slid onto the start bar, settled her skis in the tracks, checked her bindings, adjusted her helmet, and, just before she lowered her goggles, shot Mo a look.

"Ignore this," Riia whispered. "She is trying to psych you out."

Mo nodded. "Yeah, I know. I'm okay."

The start light stayed amber and Kirsti shifted her weight on the bar. Time ticked by. Even from atop the

186

hill, Mo could sense the restlessness of the people in the stands. This wasn't good for an exhibition. The light changed back to red. Kirsti's shoulders slumped and she slid over to the side, off the bar. Mo squinted at the wind speed monitor near the judges' seats, but she couldn't see the reading. The wind must have picked up, though, if they were calling Kirsti back.

The clouds above them had dropped and darkened. A handful of fat snowflakes blew by. Mo could see the officials conferring with one another.

"They will bring us down," Riia said.

Mo crossed her arms. "No, they won't. Just wait."

"But the wind—"

"The wind is going to change. It has to. We've worked too long and too hard to get here to have it end like this."

"I don't think the wind cares about how hard we have worked. If it wants to blow, it will blow."

Mo knew she was right. There was nothing she—or the officials—could do if the weather turned bad, but she didn't want to accept it. Too many things in her life were beyond her control—her parents, her love life, equality in her sport—why did the weather have to work against her, too?

Kirsti came and stood next to them. She watched the officials with a hardness in her eyes that surprised even Mo. "We will jump. If they have to wait five minutes or five hours for the wind to change, we will jump."

Fortunately, the wait time was closer to minutes than hours. The light turned amber once again and Kirsti slid back into place. A green light flashed almost before she had the chance to adjust her goggles. Mo held her breath and counted to ten. That was all the time Kirsti had to leave the bar without being disqualified. She pushed off just in time.

Mo had to admit that it was the best run she'd ever seen Kirsti do. Her takeoff was perfectly timed, her form excellent, and her landing flawless. The crowd jumped to their feet, cheering as she touched down just under the K-line. Fifty-two and a half style points and fifty-six distance. The new jump to beat.

"We're dead," Riia muttered.

Mo pressed her lips together. "Not yet."

Four more jumpers went in quick succession. It looked like the officials were determined to get the first round of jumpers through before the wind changed again. Riia flew as number ten, landing well short of the K-line. She got good style points, though. Two more jumpers and then it was Mo's turn.

Time seemed to stand still as she slid onto the start bar. She checked her bindings and adjusted her goggles and leaned forward, skis aligned in the tracks. The light turned green and the whole world narrowed to that single moment. She crouched and slid off the bar, snow hissing beneath her skis as she raced down the inrun. She anticipated the end of the ramp and sprang the instant it came into view, just as Leevi had said. And then she flew. The wind had moved, coming at her from the side more than from behind. She used one hand like a wind flap to correct her trajectory, but other than that, held her form steady. The world stilled as she hung in the air. She touched down smoothly, one foot in front of the other and glided up the outrun hill. Total adrenaline rush! It was all she could do to keep from punching the air and shouting. No matter what her distance was, she knew she nailed the style. Everything about the jump felt right. Felt good.

She turned to face the scoreboard. Yes! Fifty-four jump points—just a couple short of Kirsti's run. The style points flashed on the board. Fifty-three! With that, Mo could even take the lead in round two.

She bent to unfasten her bindings and then had to stand there while some officials came and checked the fit of her suit. She didn't understand much of what they were saying, but she knew she'd pass, thanks to Coach Peltonen's anal checking and rechecking of suits and skis. They waved her on, and she picked up her skis, nearly humming as she hiked back over to the hill for the second run.

"Great! Good job," Coach Peltonen called.

Mo looked up. Next to the coach stood Leevi, clipboard in hand. He met her eye and nodded his approval, even if he didn't quite smile. That was all she needed. Mo was grinning enough for both of them.

Kirsti earned a hundred and five total points on her second run and held on to the lead. No one had caught her by the time Mo was up. She slid onto the start bar knowing that there was a very real possibility that she, Mo, could outscore Kirsti for first place. Talk about psyching herself out! She had to forget that and make herself just go with the run. It felt almost as good as the first, but the tailwind had returned and Mo knew before she even looked that the extra drag on the back of her skis had lost her some distance. Sure enough, she had come down seven meters short of the K-line. Not enough to overtake Kirsti, but still a solid second. A pang of disappointment shot through her, but she let it go. She'd done her best, and dammit, she was not going to feel bad about that.

She undid her skis and carried them to the side, looking for Riia so they could pass the time together as they waited for the awards ceremony.

"Maureen! Maureen Clark!"

Mo searched the sea of faces.

"Over here!"

A reporter in a navy-blue parka and matching hat waved at her and pushed his way forward, cameraman in tow. "Miss Clark!"

He was American; she could tell by the Midwest accent, but she didn't recognize him as one of the regulars from the FIS circuit. Still, she switched into media mode and shook his hand.

"Bill Bouchard here from Sports News Network. You mind if we have a few minutes of your time?"

"No problem." She smiled toward the other man, who had hoisted his camera onto his shoulder and pointed it in her direction.

Mr. Bouchard rushed through an on-camera introduction and then turned his microphone on Mo. "How does it feel to be among a select few women to jump in the Lahti Ski Games?"

"Well, I didn't actually jump in the games; this is an exhibition, but I'm proud to have been a part of it."

"Would you say that this exhibition is a step toward gender equity in your sport?"

Mo smiled. "Absolutely. I hope our showing here can pave the way not only for inclusion in the Lahti Ski Games, but in the Olympics as well."

"And yours was a very nice showing, indeed—finishing second overall. I believe you topped your distance on the K120 by at least seven meters with that first jump."

She blinked in surprise. He knew her stats? Who *was* he? "Um, yeah. That sounds about right."

"So tell us, Miss Clark, how did you find those extra seven meters?"

Mo eyed Mr. Bouchard. Well, there was a lead-in if she'd ever heard one. "Excellent coaching from Coach Peltonen of the SAE, of course, and personal attention from his assistant, Leevi Patrin, who, as you may know, is also an

SAE student. You'll be seeing him jump tomorrow."

Mr. Bouchard consulted his notebook. "Leevi Patrin?"

"You got it. Believe me, he's the one to watch."

They concluded the interview just in time for the awards portion of the exhibition. Mo proudly stood on the podium to receive her token medal and bouquet of flowers. Proud not only because she had placed in the top three and earned a spot as a front-runner, but because she had kept her end of the bargain even when Leevi had deserted her. Surely that earned some kind of brownie points in heaven—or at least with Leevi . . . if she ever told him, which she probably wouldn't.

She glanced up at Kirsti, who was standing on the top platform of the podium. Mo would have thought Kirsti would be ecstatic, or at the very least pleased, to be receiving her first-place medal, but she didn't look happy. In fact, she seemed to be scowling at someone in the crowd. Mo followed Kirsti's gaze to see the Aaltos, talking and laughing with the clients they had brought to the exhibition. Her heart dropped. This was the moment Kirsti had been killing herself to show them, and they were too busy schmoozing to give her their attention.

With the awards duly given, the focus in the stadium was quickly diverted to the Nordic skiers. Coach Peltonen signaled as Mo and the others stepped down from the platform. "Go ahead and get changed," he said, "then meet back here to go over the instructions for tomorrow."

Mo changed and put her equipment away and was on her way to meet Coach Peltonen when some cell phone started playing a digitized tune. It probably went through about three rounds before she realized it was hers. She fished the phone out of her pocket.

"*Haloo? Maureen puhelimassa.*"

"Maureen? Is that you?"

"Daddy?"

"What was that you just said when you answered the phone?"

"What? I was just saying it was me." She cupped her hand over the phone. "What are you doing?"

"What do you mean, what am I doing?"

"Why are you calling? Is everything all right?"

"Maureen?"

"Mom? What's going on?"

"We're very proud of you, honey. Great job today."

"What?"

"Here's your brother."

"Yo, Mo."

"Spence? What's with the—"

"So who's this Patrin guy?"

Mo nearly dropped the phone. "What?!"

"Patrin. The assistant."

"How would you know about—"

"Nice interview, by the way. Real highlights material."

"You saw the interview?"

"Here's Mom."

"No! Talk to me! Tell me—"

"Wonderful job, honey. We're all real proud of you."

"Mom. How did you—"

"Your father wants to say good-bye. Love you, sweetheart! Buh-bye."

Her dad's voice came on the line before Mo could reply. "Well, that's everyone for now. Great job, Tiny. You did the Clark name proud."

Mo ground her teeth. "I asked you never to call me that."

"Old habits…"

"Dad. How did you see the exhibition? Are they broadcasting it in the States? I've never seen—"

"Bill has a satellite feed."

"Who?"

"Come on. You remember Bill Bouchard. Did that documentary on the school a few years back. I asked him to keep an eye on my little girl…"

All the warm fuzzies Mo had been feeling from hearing her family's voices evaporated.

"Look, Dad. I gotta go."

She turned off the phone.

The Aaltos threw a cocktail party for their big clients to celebrate Kirsti's success. Of course, Kirsti didn't know anyone there. Mo didn't either, but Herra Aalto was happy to parade her around, proudly introducing her as Kip Clark's daughter. Mo forced herself to smile and be pleasant until she noticed Kirsti slip away down the hall. She excused herself and followed.

"Kirsti?" She tapped on the bedroom door.

"Go away."

Mo stepped inside the door and shut it behind her. "Are you okay?"

Kirsti shot Mo a scathing look. "What are you doing back here? Won't your fans miss you?"

"Whatever. I just wanted to make sure you're all right."

"Oh, yes, because you're the good one. Miss Congeniality. Well, I don't need your pity."

"Pity? Hellooo. You *won.*"

"Do you think that means anything? No one really cares. You think my parents have any idea what it took to get here? The things I *did*? No!"

"What are you talking about?"

Kirsti stared at Mo for a long moment and took a deep breath. "Think about it. Why do you think that *Romalainen* boyfriend of yours stopped working with you? I did that. I talked to him when we were in Kemi. Told him that you said you could never really be interested in anyone like him—a Gypsy blood. Said you were just using him. And you know what? He believed me."

Mo's eyes grew wide. "What? But you know that's not true! Why would you...?"

Kirsti's expression turned to ice. "Welcome to the big bad world. Win at all costs; that's what it's about, right? But of course, you know all about that—sneaking around, lying to my parents. I just took it to the next level."

If ever Mo wanted to take Kirsti down, she did then. She would have, too, if it hadn't been for that bit about the sneaking around. Touché. But Kirsti was wrong. "It isn't all about winning. There are more important things."

"Not to my parents. Not to me." Kirsti's voice lost its edge. "I did what I had to do." She swiped at her eyes with the back of her hand and turned away.

Mo stared at the back of her head. "You're selling yourself short, Kirsti. You never had to do anything to win but jump."

"Don't be stupid." Kirsti's voice sounded strangled. "You don't still think this is about the jumps, do you?"

"What?"

"Don't you get it? I've had to fight all my life for my parents' attention. You weren't even here yet before my dad was fawning all over you. Everyone likes you. You even get a camera crew to follow you around. I get to be on a poster on the wall of my parents' travel agency—and they never even look at it. You know what's ironic? I have no connection with my parents, but people think they can use me to get to them." She laughed bitterly. "I figured that's what Leevi was doing to you. But he *liked* you. It didn't seem fair that you could have everything else and get the guy, too."

"So you lied to him."

Kirsti looked up. Tears filled her eyes. "Yes," she whispered.

Mo stood motionless for a long time. She didn't know what to think, let alone what to say. She left Kirsti in the room, walked past the Aaltos and their celebration, and out the door.

Nothing changes perspective like a good long think, and Mo had plenty of time for thinking as she walked along the icy sidewalk, hands buried deep in her pockets. She'd always hated the way her family dominated her life, especially her dad. But she wouldn't trade places with Kirsti. Not in a million years.

The next morning, Mo stood at the top of the big hill, fastening the bindings on her skis. Down below, thousands of spectators crowded the stadium and spilled out into the streets beyond. Through the whisper of the wind and the beating of her own heart, she could hear their excited buzz as they waited for the games to begin. Only about half of them, if that many, would be watching her make the preliminary run down the hill, but she didn't care. She wasn't in it for the crowds. In just a few minutes, she would become one of the first women in history to jump in the Lahti Ski Games.

She shivered, even though she was too keyed up to feel the cold. Her entire focus these past weeks had been to reach this point, but she hadn't anticipated what it would feel like to actually be here. She'd imagined achieving her goal would bring with it some feeling of completion, but now, with the world literally at her feet, this moment felt more like she was standing at a starting gate than crossing a finish line. From here, anything was possible.

Kirsti nudged Mo's arm timidly. "You ready for this?" After the revelation last night, Kirsti didn't seem to know quite how to act. Mo could tell she was trying her hardest to be nice. It was almost amusing how difficult that seemed to be, or might have been if it wasn't so sad.

Sadder still was how hard it was for Mo to be nice back. Mo hated what Kirsti had done. Hated it! But she couldn't dwell on the negative energy. Not if she was going to jump her best. She forced a smile. "I'm ready."

"Good, because you're up."

Mo took a deep breath and slid onto the start bar. Trembling, she settled her skis in the tracks and adjusted her goggles.

"Relax!" Kirsti called. "You're going to do great!"

Mo smiled for real this time, and shook the tension from her shoulders. It was all about the jump. Nothing else mattered. The amber light turned green and she slid away from the bar.

Flying from the hill, she never felt so free.

• • •

Mo watched the men's competition and was pleased to see Leevi come in fifth overall in the men's event. Not bad, considering the world-class level of the competition. It was an accomplishment for him to place. Mo couldn't help but notice Bill Bouchard and his crew standing by after Leevi had received his certificate. She smiled. All was as it should be.

Almost.

Mo waited in the crowded hallway outside the guys' locker room when the competition was over. She must have looked like some rabid groupie or something, but she didn't care; she had to talk to Leevi.

She ran the words she wanted to say to him over and over in her head, but when Leevi finally emerged through the door, her perfect speech evaporated. All she could do was blurt, "Kirsti was wrong!"

He stopped midstep and stared at her. When he opened his mouth to speak, she shook her head. "No. Let me finish. Kirsti lied to keep you from helping me. I don't have a problem with you being *Roma* and I can prove it." With that, she stepped up to him, grabbed his face in both hands, and kissed him on the lips right in front of everybody. It made her feel all bubbly and tingly and out of breath... and suddenly very shy. Slowly she became aware of the hoots and jeers from the other guys who were coming out of the room. She let go and stepped back.

Leevi regarded her for a moment, unsmiling. Mo's heart dropped. He was still mad. He didn't like public displays of affection. He—

"Kirsti told me," he said.

"No, but she was wrong. I don't really—"

Leevi pulled Mo close to him. He kissed her, slow and deep. Now she really couldn't breathe. Her stomach did aerials as her heart danced a samba. She wanted to laugh and shout...but not now. Right now she just wanted to kiss him back.

"Kirsti told me what she did," he said at last. "She talked to me this morning."

Mo was speechless. And not because she couldn't catch her breath, either. Kirsti confessed?

"I tried to find you," he said.

Mo could only nod. He still had his arms around her and she decided at that moment that nothing else mattered.

Mo and Leevi walked hand in hand through the sculpture park. More than once, Leevi asked if she would rather go someplace indoors—someplace where she wouldn't freeze.

Each time, she smiled and shook her head. "No, I like it here." She loved that he had thought to take her to the park—the site of their first "date."

"So what next, Clark? Any big plans when you get home?"

Her smile evaporated. She didn't want to think about leaving. She shrugged. "Oh, you know. Fight the IOC. Jump in the next Olympics. That sort of thing. What about you? Where do you want to go to school?"

"Anywhere that I can keep training. I've applied to about ten different schools."

"You think it will make a difference?" She didn't want to say what she meant. When he came back to Finland, wouldn't the same discrimination still exist?

"Yeah. I do. Sometimes you just have to get away and prove to everyone what you can do."

She nodded. That she understood.

"And things change, you know? It was even harder for my parents. My dad was the first one in his family to go to university. I'll be the fifth in mine."

"So what are you going to major in?"

"Mechanical engineering."

Giving him a sideways glance, she smiled. She wouldn't have expected that, but by now she knew you could never tell what someone was really like, just from looking at them from the outside. Kinda like the snow-covered statues in the park. Mo nodded to herself. Now she understood why Leevi liked them so much.

Mo closed her suitcase and took one last look around Kirsti's room. Weird as it sounded, she was going to miss it here.

Herra Aalto knocked at the door. "Are you ready to go?"

"Almost. I just need to, uh..." She looked meaningfully in the direction of the WC.

"Ah. Well, we'll wait for you in the front room."

As soon as he was gone, Mo slipped a small box out from under her pillow. She set it on Kirsti's computer desk and propped up a card beside it. She turned away, suddenly feeling stupid, and looked up to see Kirsti at the door, watching her.

"Oh." Now Mo felt really dumb. "I didn't see you there."

Kirsti shrugged and gave her half a smile. "I came to say good-bye before I left."

Mo nodded. The local students had school that day. She felt a little sad about not being able to say good-bye to everyone one last time, but on the other hand, it was probably easier this way. Mo never was one for good-byes.

"What's that?" Kirsti asked.

Mo blushed. "Oh, it's just...I wanted to tell you thanks for sharing your room."

"Oh. You're...welcome."

Mo picked up the box and held it out to her. "Here. It's not much, just..."

Kirsti took the gift and sat on the bed to open it. She pulled the roseolive kivi from the paper. "Your candle," she whispered.

Mo sat beside her and took the votive from her hand.

She held it to the light. "I liked this one because of the way the color changes. You can see something new whenever you look at it in a different light." She hoped Kirsti would know what she meant.

Kirsti took the kivi and stared at it. "You'd better go." Her voice sounded husky.

Mo gathered her things and rolled the suitcase across the room. She was nearly out the door when Kirsti called out to her. *"Kiitos."*

Herra Aalto left Mo at the Sports Center parking lot, where the SAE exchange students met to board the bus bound for the airport.

She dropped into her seat and waved good-bye through the window. Blinking back tears, she took one last look at the ski hills. Someday she'd be back. Maybe for the World Championships—and by then, women would be a real part of the games. The doors hissed as they closed and the bus lumbered over the ruts in the ice on the parking lot. The hills slowly disappeared into the distance.

Mo watched the buildings and forests roll by the window one last time, trying to memorize every last tree. Cars and trucks passed the bus in the other lane, as did some poor guy on a motorcycle. Who'd want to ride a motorcycle in this weather was beyond—Mo sat straight up. She knew that jacket. Leevi! He waved, then pulled ahead of the bus and sped off down the road.

The rest of the ride, Mo couldn't sit still. She fidgeted, zipping and unzipping her backpack and applying lip gloss only to wipe it off again. Finally they reached the airport and pulled up to the departure curb. It was all she could do to wait her turn and act casual as she got off the bus.

Leevi was waiting just inside the door. Mo shook her head as she walked toward him. "You're crazy, do you know that?"

He just smiled, which made her want to melt right there in the airport lobby.

"I need to, um..." She gestured at her suitcase. He nodded and stood with her in the check-in line. Neither of them said much until her suitcase was safely in the hands of the airline and Mo had her boarding pass in hand.

"I can't believe it's over," Mo said finally. "I was just getting used to you."

He shook his head. "It's not over. Remember, there are no endings, only beginnings."

She laughed. "Where'd you find that one? The Cliché Handbook?"

Coach Peltonen had been keeping a respectful distance, but cleared his throat as he approached. "Sorry, Mo, but it's time. The group is waiting on the other side of security."

Mo took a deep breath. "Well, I guess this is it."

Leevi nodded.

"Thanks for everything," she said.

He nodded again.

"Okay, well…" She took a step back.

"Mo."

"Yeah?"

He wrapped an arm around her and kissed her one last time. His lips were still cold from the motorcycle ride, but they managed to make her feel all warm inside.

Mo smiled shakily when he let go. "Bye," she managed, then turned and ran for the security line before the lump in her throat developed into tears.

On the plane, Mo stuffed her backpack into the overhead bin. She took off her coat and was about to shove it up there, too, when she felt something crinkle in the pocket. Her hands shook as she pulled out an envelope. It was from Leevi. She dropped into her seat and tore it open.

Just wanted to let you know, he wrote, *I got a scholarship to the Colorado Mountain College so I'll be training in Steamboat Springs. See you on the circuit.*

Mo settled back in her seat and smiled. No endings, he'd said. She refolded the note, tucking it carefully back into her pocket. Now she had another finish line to work toward—the USSA SuperTour. Last stop, Steamboat Springs, Colorado.

And that was just the beginning.

For more about Women's Ski Jumping,
turn the page for a special note
from author Linda Gerber.

When I began writing this book, the 2006 Winter Olympics had just gotten under way in Torino, Italy, and the women's ski jumping team out of Park City, Utah, was on fire, featuring five of the top fifteen women's jumpers in the world. Unfortunately, one had little to do with the other since women ski jumpers were not allowed to compete in the Olympics.

Throughout the following year, I watched as these athletes, their colleagues, and Women's Ski Jumping USA launched an aggressive campaign to allow the women athletes the same opportunities as their male counterparts. They appealed to the International Ski Federation (FIS) and the International Olympic Committee (IOC) to step into the twenty-first century and include women ski jumpers in world class and Olympic competition.

One by one, the barriers standing in the way of Olympic inclusion were broken down. An official who had claimed that ski jumping "seem(ed) not to be appropriate for ladies from a medical point of view" retracted his silly statement. VISA continued its leadership of women's athletics by stepping forward as a corporate sponsor. The FIS approved a world championship in 2009 for women's ski jumping. Five women jumpers were named to the US Ski Team. At long last, all signs pointed to Olympic inclusion for women.

In November 2006, the IOC met in Kuwait City to vote. They decided to exclude women ski jumpers yet again in the 2010 Olympics.

Attempting to reverse this decision, Canadian athletes appealed to the Human Rights Commission and filed an official complaint in February 2007, citing gender bias.

As of the printing of this book, the IOC decision stands.

You can read more about women's ski jumping and the fight for Olympic inclusion at **www.wsjusa.com**.